THE AVATARS

THE AVATARS

A FUTURIST FANTASY

BY

A. E.

The Light is the real person in the picture.
CLAUD MONET

CORACLE PRESS

San Rafael, Ca

Second, Facsimile edition,
Coracle Press, 2008
First edition, Macmillan and Co., 1933

For information, address:
Coracle Press, P.O. Box 151011
San Rafael, California 94915, USA

Library of Congress Cataloging-in-Publication Data

AE, 1867–1935.
The avatars: a futurist fantasy / A. E. — 2nd, facsim. ed.
p. cm.
ISBN 978-1-59731-303-2 (alk. paper)
ISBN 978-1-59731-302-5 (pbk.: alk. paper)
1. Avatars (Religion)—Fiction. I. Title.

PR6035.U7A9 2008
823'.912—dc22 2008021929

TO

W. B. YEATS

THERE is no imagination of mine about Avatars in this book. No more than an artist could paint the sun at noon could I imagine so great beings. But as a painter may suggest the light on hill or wood, so in this fantasy I tried to imagine the spiritual excitement created by two people who pass dimly through the narrative, spoken of by others but not speaking themselves. I have, I fear, delayed too long the writing of this, for as I grow old the moon of fantasy begins to set confusedly with me. *The Avatars* has not the spiritual gaiety I desired for it. The friends with whom I once spoke of such things are dead or gone far from me. If they were with me, out of dream, vision and intuition shared between us, I might have made the narrative to glow. As it is, I have only been able to light my way with my own flickering lantern.

A. E.

I

In the winter twilight a young man was flying from civilisation. His way lay between many snow-covered hills. Why was he flying from city to mountain? On the morning of that wintry day his city had appeared to him to be an evil wrought by sorcerers, who, at the close of their labours, had summoned fog, gloom and cold, a grey consistory, to intervene between the heart and heaven. He had watched from his window dejected figures looming and vanishing in the fog, their world a blur of grey mist above, a blur of murky brown underfoot. He had thought for an instant a picture might be made of these sad shadows darkling and fading in the cloudy air, but shrank from the idea of giving permanence to what was not in itself desirable life. A wind had swept the fog from the street, but the thinning mist revealed only the dull darkness of the houses opposite, in bleak unlikeness to the City the artist imagination would build on earth.

"It must be sorcery keeps the world as it is," he had thought. And fancy had created a vivid grotesque, a council of wizards riding high on the steely air, monstrous shapes with eyes opaque as stone, like to that fabled Balor of the Evil Eye, but petrifying hearts, not bodies, with a glance. If not like these in body, like these in soul must have been the creators of that dark industrial architecture which made a gloom in the air. He thought of the minds darkened in those mills, face and form losing comeliness, the mechanical eliminating use of the joyous creative faculty. He had himself been manacled to the mechanical world when a boy. He recalled his agony at the dimming of imaginative life in dull labours; an agony which one day grew unendurable, and impelled him there and then to escape, prepared to let body starve rather than soul. The exaltation of revolt carried him far from the city, a vagabond truly, but happy, restored to the everlasting companions, air and light, who flung their arms about him. He had journeyed on and on over an earth rich with lakes and woods, with noons misty with light, and mountains that in the evening seemed to ascend in flame. They were all calling him to be of their brotherhood. It was then he first felt their beauty was transparent. Some being, remote yet intimate, peered at him from the deeps of air. The apparitions of light, cloud, mountain and wood underwent a transfiguration into life, a vaster remoter self or oversoul to his own being. So, spell-stricken, he had passed from wonder to wonder, until at last the western sea stayed his travelling. There he met Michael Conaire, who became to him an elder brother; and, by his help, Paul came to be the artist which was nature's intent for him. The thought of that old friend had come to him in his despondency as light draws the lost traveller in some midnight valley. With an impetuous obedience to impulse in which he never failed, he had hastened to pack up the materials of his art. In his hurrying mind the air was shining, the foam was leaping, the snow was pure on mountain and field, the fire was on the hearth and the whimsical elder was beside it, all that would meet him at the end of his journey. So he started on his second flight from civilisation. An hour after the dull city and its melancholy slaves were behind him. He wondered if time would ever come when they would revolt as he had done, return to nature and let that mother restore their lost likeness in soul and body to the ancestral beauty. Only a god, he thought, could arouse them from their stupor. As he drew nigh at twilight to that western land he loved, half in a dream he watched from the silently running car the fields white without a gleam; the hills a chilly violet against a sky of lemon light; the cottages on the hillside; tall smoke rising up through stillest air; here and there a glint of gold from door or window. It was all so pure and cold and lovely that he closed his eyes to lay it reverently in the chamber of beautiful memories. Then his mood of half dream became wholly dream, and passed into trance, and vision came strangely to him with power and the sense of purpose.

In that illumination of vision he was brought to a cottage on some mountainside. He knew not where. He saw, by a light in himself which made the dusk lucid, the snow pale as pearl lying on rock and ridge and roof with a blue lustre taken from a sky with just awakening stars. One window only was aglow piercing the whitewashed walls, and about that homestead a delicate nimbus was spread as if rayed from a lovely life hidden within. Above the cottage rose two watchers, crested with many-coloured lights, gigantic forms that seemed shaped from some burnished and exquisite fire. They held swords of wavering flame as if guardians of some precious thing.

There was gentleness amid the awe the vision created: and it was all marvellously clear, clearer than anything imagination had ever beheld and beyond his own imagination beautiful.

Paul opened his eyes and, starting up, he looked wildly about him, but he could see nothing but the dark ridged mountains rising on either side of the valley road. The only lights were the stars and the far lights of homes on the hillside, and he knew not where to search for that cottage of wonder. He sank back, closing his eyes that he might see again, but the vision had vanished, and memory could not recreate it in its first magical lustre. He groaned in himself that he should have started up and had lost maybe some further revelation. The car ran on along the snowy road, the driver, unconscious of the mad imaginations of his silent passenger, hurrying him from the valley of vision. At last there came a twist in the road, and then the shadowy shining of a lake below battlements of rock, and beyond that dim sea, and beyond that still dimmer mountains. Paul recalled his thoughts from their wild careering as the car turned into an avenue. In a moment he was before an open door; there was a hall ruddy with light and a figure with arms uplifted in welcome.

II

"Dear Paul, I felt at midday you were coming. You sent your thought flying before you. I have been looking along the road for an hour or more." Behind Conaire was his wife, kind as himself, the silent and affectionate listener to interminable rhapsody and speculation from the talkative philosopher. Conaire was radiant in the anticipation of a less silent hearer. He foresaw colloquies stretching beyond midnight with the artist he had fostered. That night truly he was stirred as Paul hesitatingly told of the vision in the dark valley. Conaire sat up quivering with excitement.

"There is a prologue in heaven to that," he began impressively. "I know now why I met you seven years ago. I know why you revolted against the mechanical. I know why you and I are what we are. I know why Lavelle fashioned poetry out of legend and coloured it with fairy. I know why Brehon turned to a language which had become almost a tradition, and why the enthusiasts of a rural civilisation began their labours. They were all forerunners. Now there will be spiritual adventures, knights-errant, dragons to be slain, black magic and divine enchantments. I would not now exchange this my age for any other; not to sit at the Banquet and hear the wisdom of Socrates: not to be in Babylon with the great king: not to see Solomon bewitch the Queen of Sheba!"

"Incurable romantic! Tell me about the prologue in heaven," said Paul, amused and pleased as all are when thought of theirs is taken by another, and the psychic juggler tosses it in the air, and it breaks out into many shining forms with faces looking in every direction. It was to warm himself at this glow of fancy he had fled from the city. "I came here to have my gloom lit up by the torch of your mind. Begin in heaven, dear friend, and you can descend by way of the half-gods to the hearth where I sit. Make the journey as long as you like. I am excited about that aureoled cottage with its watchers. I never dreamed earth had such fiery gigantic citizens. My being leaped up in light when I saw them. Do you think it more than imagination?"

"It is not imagination. It is seership. Listen, Paul. When I was young the whole world was at war, as you know. You could not remember the agony but you know the black night which settled on men's souls after it. I thought the Iron Age was to be with us for ever, that beauty was to be but a memory, that earth deserted by the gods was to spin desolate in space. You know what infinite sorrow the heart can feel when we are young. In the midnight of my despair I too had a vision. My sleep broke into a dazzle of light, and I was raised above myself to be with the immortals. They glimmered starlike about me, each in the image by which they were fabled. They were gazing silently at a ruddy divinity who was waving his hand from the heaven world at the troubled earth. It was Ares, proud, for he had drawn men in millions to act in his greatest drama. The gentler deities held counsel together. The memory of that tragedy must be obliterated. The curtain of blackness which would fall when it was over must be lifted on a new drama to be enacted, a drama like one of the beautiful plays of antiquity in which gods took part as hero or heroine. Such was the play of Helen which made men realise that beauty was a divinity. Such was the play of Radha and Krishna which taught lovers how to evoke god and goddess in each other. Only a deity could undo what a deity had done. So now there must be born on earth divine shepherds to lead men back to ancient happiness and beauty. The immortals, gazing on earth, communed as to where the incarnation would take place. In the Old World the hearts of men were so heavy that they could not be uplifted even by a god. In the New World the hearts of men were so fierce that not even the power of the immortals could save their avatar if he did not worship the idols men had there set up. There was India always ready to prostrate itself before a divinity. But India had many avatars, and if a new avatar came it would still be prostrate and gentle and would not rise up in pride. Then one pointed to a land where lived a perfectly impossible people with whom anything was possible. And when he had pointed it out, all the immortals turned their eyes and looked on me and I awoke."

"Your imagination leaps by the tipsiest stepping-stones from darkness to light and with seven-leagued boots," said Paul, contrary from old custom, yet all the while willing to be convinced life's darkness could be transmuted into precious fires. "But if you took any two dreams by any two other people and made them stepping-stones for your seven-leagued imagination, into what incredible regions in space and time would you not be carried?"

"There are not two stepping-stones only. But by treading on these I can see the stepping-stones behind me and others ahead," Conaire answered, delighted at an opposition which was a signal to summon up whole legions of theory. "My vision doubtless appears to you more personal fantasy than an image of truth. But truth may be revealed in symbol. When we fall asleep after a day of anxiety our desires often dramatise themselves in dream which is a true symbol of our waking state. The circumstance of the dream may be incredible. What it symbolises is a truth. In the secrecy of sleep, in that state we call dreamless, we wake to a life of divine reality. When we emerge from that state its realities may dramatise themselves in symbolic dreams, and these realities must drape themselves in whatever shapes they can find. The circumstance of the dream may be incredible and yet the idea symbolised may be worthy philosophic scrutiny. I know," continued Conaire with a deprecating movement of hands and features, "my mind is encrusted with fantasies. I built them up as a defence against the grey folk who were ever assailing me with the wish that I become as colourless as themselves. For that habit of mind the penalty is, I receive truth only through a mist of fantasy. But I have come to believe my dream, however fantastic, mirrored some reality in divine consciousness brooding on the future, devising religions, philosophies, arts, sciences and civilisations, and breathing forth the moods by which acceptance is made possible. I think your vision was of some reality while mine was symbolic. You must not think of gods or avatars as fountains only of theological piety. In the ancient world any around whom nations pivoted to new destinies were regarded as avatars. So the goddess was surmised in Helen, the god in Alexander or Cuchulain. You must not allow your mind to be dominated by traditions of the avatars of theology. Plato says if there be any gods they certainly do not philosophise, and I am equally certain they are not like even the saintliest of archbishops. They are, I fancy, more like poets who live their own lordly imaginations. It is not an incredible speculation that one of these divine poets has taken a body in this world, and is now as child or man in that aureoled cottage on the mountainside. Are not the greater poets half gods, and why should we shrink from belief in one who is fully conscious of his divinity?"

"I would undertake labours like those of Hercules to learn the truth about my dream," cried Paul. "But what have the gods been doing since the Council in Heaven? Tell me about the forerunners. You have a segment of the divine circle, and I expect an imagination like yours to complete the full orb for me."

"It is not so easy as that," returned the philosopher. "An ancient scripture says, 'The Wise Ones guard well the home of Nature's order. They assume excellent forms in secret.' Whatever happens I am sure will be surprising however we speculate. Ares is the only diety who repeats himself. The warrior mind in heaven as on earth is devoid of imagination. Was there ever clearer evidence of flagging invention than in the Russian revolution following the French? The *dramatis personae* were the same in both dramas. A half-witted king, a haughty queen, angry philosophers, magicians, charlatans, ferocious dictators, *jacquerie* and peasant wars. But it is a fascinating subject for speculation how, after thought in Heaven on the affairs of Earth, the Divine Will might be transmuted into earthly activities. The ancients spoke of Fountains welling out of Hecate, by which symbols they expressed their belief that from the heart of divine nature there was a ceaseless flow of spiritual energy on all that live. In many lands there are legends of these sidereal Fountains—in our own country also. It was by breathing the exhalations from mystic nature the Sibyls were inspired to prophecy. This indicated the belief of the ancients that ideas born in the Heaven world descended to the Earth dwellers by these ethereal streams. We can imagine one of these Fountains feeding with spiritual vitality the people among whom the incarnation is to take place, first coloured by the presence of the god; and the spiritually sensitive, awakened to a new consciousness by the current laving heart and mind, stirred to give it expression and so becoming forerunners of the Avatar. These naturally would seek symbols and affinities in myth, legend and tradition of ages when this commerce between Heaven and Earth was understood. What is spoken of as the mystic paganism of our poets is not merely a protest against mechanical life, but is the desire of the soul to live amid its spiritual affinities. The very names they use, the names of ancient gods and heroes, have a power of evocation. Those who, allured by the magic of rhythm, murmur these names, whether they know it or not, are weaving spells and incantations. The powers evoked flow to them out of the Ever Living. The earth is changed for them; and all this prepares the way for the Avatar; for, if there were no forerunners, there would be none who could understand his voice. The forerunners arouse ideas latent in the character of the people. The Avatar wakens these to full consciousness and indicates their final goal. The purpose of an Avatar is to reveal the spiritual character of a race to itself."

"Can you say of us that we do not know our own spiritual character?" asked Paul.

"Do you know when you listen to orchestra what next shall follow on the music sounding on the air, whether flute or violin shall most intoxicate the sense? But whatever instrument dominates, if the work be by a great master, we feel the sequence was inevitable even if unforeseen. The master knows the quality of the instrument and its full tones. We do not know until the master has played on the instrument what music it can make. We do not know ourselves but we are known. The spiritual cultures we associate with Greece, Egypt, India, Persia, China or Judea were all in the divine consciousness before they were in the human. I can imagine, before the awakening of Greece, before a poet had sung to a lyre or a statue was carved, the Lords of the world, who know what is within, perceiving the latent instinct for beauty, and that some divine messenger incarnated to be its Avatar. It may have been that being, fabled long after as Apollo, by whom was awakened that consciousness which culminated in epic, drama, statue, temple; and which realised its divine origin in a philosophy which declared that Deity was Beauty in its very essence. Can we say of our own people what one mood is dominant, as we can say in ancient Greece there was the passion for beauty, or in ancient India there was the longing for spiritual truth?"

"But," said Paul, "you came out of that high conclave with the thought we were an impossible people. Why, if that be so, should everything be possible?"

"The marriage of Heaven and Earth has not taken place here as among the races I have mentioned," returned the philosopher placidly. "Where it has taken place men can live by reason. We have not that rational life. We live by intuition or instinct. At times our life is golden. At other times we are like demons from Eblis."

"I am in a mood to believe anything to-night," said Paul. He moved about the room restless as the orange-glow dancing and dwindling on the wall, an echo in light of the ruddy hearth. Then he went to the window and looked out on a mountainous earth, all blue, fairy and still in its mask of snow. It seemed more imagination than reality. The sky leaning over the lofty crags was like a face all majesty of expression yet without features. The sense of it being living overcame him. It seemed to draw nearer and nearer, to be at the window, intense with spirit being. The window for an instant was a portal into eternity. He came back to Conaire. "I do not understand myself. I know nothing about life. This morning I felt as if iron bars were to close about us for ever and I hurried here like the condemned escaping from a dungeon. To-night I feel as if I had but to lift my hands and call 'Be ye lifted up, ye everlasting doors,' and that apparition of earth and sky would be rolled up as a curtain. But," he said dejectedly, "they would not be lifted up. We are only children tilting at unassailable walls."

"It is in the awakening of an eye the dead

shall be raised," said Conaire. "Was it with those eyes you saw the fiery watchers on the hillside? I think you are a natural seer, but you have been content as an artist with the images you created for yourself. An Eastern sage said we could climb into Heaven by brooding on knowledge which came in dream. If you brood on your vision it may start you on some marvellous travelling. Remember the Persian poet:

> a single Alif were the clue,
> Could we but find it, to the Treasure House
> And peradventure to the Master too."

III

A MOOD at once gay and solemn is born in the soul when it first discovers a path to light out of the dark cavern of the body, and is made aware of wide realms to travel in with a higher order of beings as companions. Such a mood overwhelmed Paul when he laid his head on a pillow and closed his eyes to sleep. He found, not the accustomed shade into which consciousness fades, but a jewel lustre as if whatever being had imparted to him its own vision, by that momentary commerce with him had made everything radiant, leaving behind it shining memories of its own nature and its travel from Heaven to Earth.

In that mood of mingled awe and exaltation Paul pursued the trail of glittering images. He seemed to himself to be borne up on a river of luminous and living air, and to be carried in vision into the heart of a great mountain. When he had passed within there was no hill, but a dazzle of light cast up from some interior fountain. He was aware of lofty beings there, kinsmen of those fiery watchers who kept guard on the mountain ridges. He did not feel anything was strange, for he seemed to have some ancient knowledge of it all. There was a spirit in him, too, deeper than conscious thought, which knew of a vaster life beyond all vision. He would have drawn nigher those lordly ones, but there was some constraint on him which he could not break, and at last there came relaxing of the will and he slept. It may have been that spirit within him desired to part from the waking self before it passed through the gateway of light to high adventures of its own. However it may have been, when Paul awoke he felt inexpressibly young and happy as if he had been reborn and baptized with some glorious fire. His limbs were light to move, and his fancies like a gay multitude of fish, flying to and fro, sunlit in water. He dressed and went out, climbing the snow-covered ridge that rose behind the house, so that his eyes might drink in all his heart loved. The world without, like his world within, was all radiance in the dawn. The sea was a waste of quivering light. The lake was frozen silver. In the mountainous lands the heights were glittering with gold, and the hollows blue, lustrous and ethereal as the abyss of air overhead. Here and there was a starry sparkling as of diamonds and opals scattered in the light. Here and there were patches of dark grey or purple or green rock, vestiges of the rugged country he knew before, but now veiled by the purity and frailty of snow. He breathed with delight the clear, cold, life-giving air. Every atom in his being was fiery. Never did he feel charged with so intense a vitality. He interpreted the universe by his own being and had the sense of life throughout dense infinitudes. He lifted up his hands crying out as one spirit to another, as if he knew in those wide spaces there was that which could hear him and could answer to his call. Then he heard a shout and saw a ruddy little figure, Conaire's only child, flying to him over the snow. She flung herself on the young artist whom she loved. Paul lifted the girl in his arms and, talking gaily to her, went back to the house.

IV

What was told of that mystic Babylon of the Apocalypse, the haunt of every unclean spirit, might have been spoken of the cities of the Iron Age dominated by the dark mechanic genius. They were haunted by yet more evil divinities and knew it not. The stars were not darkened over them. The sun shone on their streets. The clouds were snowy and spiritual as of old. All the tapestry of the heavenly house hung and flamed overhead, but there was midnight about them in Anima Mundi. In vain was the wealth created bartered for beauty. It could not purchase a light by which the soul could see it, and because of that psychic night, what was lovely to the eyes could not make gay the soul. As there are houses haunted by the shades of those who in them have done evil, so were the cities haunted by evil memories. The shades grew thicker about them through centuries as the ocean of life bathing them became more impregnated by the emanations of men leprous with sensuality, blind with fear or smouldering with hate. The larvae of the dead hung about the living with unsatiated passion, and a base desire was never solitary, for it summoned up legions of evil affinities to urge it to its consummation. As the lights of the soul became extinguished, its darkened halls and corridors were thronged by sinister inhabitants breathing animalism and corruption. They held revelry within and hence came frenzies, obsessions and unappeasable desires. The body, possessed by the shades, was made meet for its inhabitants. The character of the goat, the hog and the rat began to appear in men's faces and to efface the divine signature. In the Babylons of the ancient earth there was beauty and magnificence even of sin. Beauty was born in their courts and byways because mechanical devices had not yet been set to do the work of man. The imagination was still artificer, and the slave might hold commerce with heaven and be a creator at his labours. But, as the demon of the mechanical began to dominate the cities of the Iron Age, it brought life itself into subservience to it. The looms of the soul became silent and rich webs of fantasy no longer poured from them. The potter no more shaped his vessel with delight, moulding about it the dancing figures which were in his heart. No song sounded over labour, for the machine chanted its iron dronings by day and by night, and the sorcery made men to forget the soul had once been as illuminated as nature. The heart was ever heavy, and few were those who could hold back the gloom by creating their own light. The imagination could no more conceive of lordly life, and multitudes fell blindly into a mould devised that society might have the precision of the machine. The artificers of this vast degradation wrought on the unillumined nature so that, if any had the dream of freedom, they were made to seem the enemies of all by which men lived. By identity of character souls become welded together in the psychic world, and tend there to become entities, beings made out of multitudes, the dominant passion as soul moving all to act together as a single being. To the divine vision these cities of the Iron Age appeared as monstrous beasts, the dragon devourers of virgin life. Unable themselves to give birth to vital beings, they became insatiable vampires drawing youth out of nature to themselves to replace the life which became so rapidly burnt out, so decadent and decrepit, that none could trace ancestry beyond a grandsire who had been born in the cities.

As the cities exercising this magnetic power grew more thronged the country became more desolate and deserted. The Earth itself for leagues about them suffered a blight so that there was less magic in woodland or glade. These seemed empty of their elemental populace, dryad and hamadryad, the gentle silvery presences blowing their horns, or making with childlike voices melodies with no passion or pain in them; or else the power to see and hear these had been lost and a world of ethereal beauty had drifted beyond human cognisance. It was in one of the blackest of these cities Paul had heard a voice like that which cried in the mythic Babylon, "Come out of her, my people," and had fled away from it to hear the voice of the Earth Spirit, to listen to its multitudinous meditation, and to be inspired to become one of its instruments so that the spirit might not pass forgotten from the minds of men.

V

As a cloud fades leaving bare the fields of heaven, so the cloud of snow crumbled from rock, hill and hollow. Summer came, and Paul, still under the enchantment, lingered in the western land. Such moods of majesty and sweetness arose in him that he felt omnipresence was working the same miracles in his soul that it wrought out of earth, turning dark clay into the brilliance of leaf and flower. Nothing that lived close to the earth could altogether escape the wizardry. There was a spirit in the wild people who lived among the hills which was not in the people of the cities. They belonged, however remotely, to some mystic empire. The dullest peasant might break silence with a phrase in which the mountains seemed to speak rather than a man. Even in their orgies there was a leaven of imagination, and a spiritual light glowed, however fitfully, amid the bestial as a star might glow in the darkness of a tarn. Daily Paul was discovering the affinity between these people, himself and that mystic nature. In a late twilight he sat on a rock above a mountain road. From that twilight nigh the earth the night rose up from one blue heaven to another, and he stayed gazing through the night until his soul became one with the stillness, prolonging his reverie until it seemed to become part of the reverie of Earth itself or to take colour from its imaginations. An incoherent babbling broke the silence. It came from a man staggering along the road below. That drunken babble outraged the solemn ceremonial whereby the Lights nightly unveil the infinitude which is the symbol of God, and the Ivory Gate seemed to close at the sound. Then there was again silence, and Paul, peering through the dusk, saw the drunkard had fallen in the middle of the road. He clambered down from his seat on the rocks; and, as he bent to lift the fallen man out of danger from any cart which might pass in the darkness, he heard a half-inarticulate crooning and caught the words of an old song full of gentleness and beauty: "She passed the sally garden on little snow-white feet," and Paul knew that, through the fever and blind disorder of the reeling senses, the soul of that man was following images which were quiet and lovely, and it too belonged to the mystic empire.

Paul had brooded on that rocky ridge night after night, for he was painting the mountain which rose beyond the wooded valley and the long lake, and he carried memory of shadowy form and dim illumination to the hours of light when he could work. One morning he brought his picture to the rocky seat to compare the forms revealed by day with his memory of them shrouded in the summer night. As he brooded on the picture he felt a quickening of imagination. He closed his eyes and he saw again the huge mountain in the dim night, but now a light glowed above the high plateau and wavering flames streamed up into the air. His fingers began to quiver as if what he had imagined had run from head to hand, and he took the brushes and began to paint that mystic light above the high land. He was inspired by something beyond himself. The hand moved almost without guidance from the mind. Yet when he had ended, the psychic illumination on the mountain did not appear alien to earth but a portion of natural beauty.

"What is that light on the hill?" asked an eager and imperative voice. Paul turned. He had never seen a more beautiful boy than this who stood before him. The sunlight through the yellow curls made them glow like an aura of fire. The eyes, strange, innocent and intense, were like pools of blue light in the shadowed face. Paul's own eyes remained fixed on the boy and he could not move them, so stricken was he with that beauty. The child of a peasant, he thought. What a wonder. He might be tending sheep, but no sheep were visible.

"I do not know," he answered at last, for the boy's eyes dazzled him, and his mind was confused as the mind is oft-times by the eyes of women. "I imagined it there. It might be a palace of the Sidhe who were the old gods of our people. You may have heard of them."

"Old people speak of them," said the boy. "I have not seen them though they call me a changeling."

"Why do they call you that?" asked Paul.

"I will not do the things they wish me to do. I will not be made to learn like the others. I will not be shut out of the air. I run away."

"Do you not want to know what others know?" asked Paul.

"I know what they think," answered the boy. "They have no light in their minds unless I blow into them. Then I can make them think what I will."

"What do you make them do?" asked Paul, amused at the young dictator whose years might number twelve or fourteen. He thought the boy might indeed move people to do anything by his beauty.

"I imagine them wearing gay colours and they begin to wear them. I imagine them dancing in curves like the clouds and they begin to dance," said the boy.

Paul, who was now in imagination devising a picture of the lad as a shepherd on the hills, and who wished to know where he could find him again, asked, "What is your name?"

"Aodh," answered the boy.

"I have not seen you before. Where do you live?"

The boy waved a hand to a ridge made faint and blue by many miles of air and heat and light.

"There!" he said. "It was to see the sea I came here."

"So far!" said Paul. "How tired you must be!"

The boy laughed, and before Paul could find words to delay him he ran up the hill as lightly as another might run down. Paul saw the golden curls in a last flashing against the blue sky as the light figure leaped over the ridge of rock. I am sure to meet him again, he thought; but many years were to pass before he again saw Aodh.

VI

THE boy went on lightly leaping from rock to rock, choosing always the high ridges for his path. He had delight in his airy leapings like to that the soul feels when it wakes in dream and is buoyed on air and exults, because the vast dragging of earth no more ties its feet to heath or stone, and it can, though wingless, wander at its will like a bird. In fancy this tireless child thought of leaping from crest to crest of the long blue waves of hills. Why could he not do it? He imagined the run and the mad gathering of power for the leap, and in the very act of imagining he had left the body behind. What had happened? The air in which he floated was vibrant with timeless melody, a sound as beautiful and universal as the light. Where was he? Earth was vanishing, swallowed up in a brightness fiery as the sun, and mountains, crags and vales were fading from vision as if consumed by the ecstasy of the fire. A moment more and he would have passed from the illusion of boyhood. He was reaching up to some immeasurable power which was himself when consciousness faded. When it awoke again he heard voices speaking above him.

"It is time to awaken him. The seer cannot be held to the eyes. The being cannot be tied to the body."

He looked up. He saw a figure thrice the height of mortals, a body gleaming as if made of golden and silver airs. It was winged with flame above the brows. The eyes which looked on him were still as if they had gazed only on eternities, and the boy cried and knew not why he uttered the words.

"I know you, Shepherd of the Starry Flocks. What soul do you now draw from the abyss?"

There were others, a high companionship, but he saw only for an instant a light of calm and lordly faces, and the next instant he was standing on the mountain grass, his limbs still bent for the leap he had imagined. He shook his ruddy curls in perplexity as he looked about him. The air was still and empty of sound or light, save the light from the far fire in the sky, and it seemed a grey twilight to the light which had vanished. "The sun is dark to-day," he said to himself. He felt a chill which was spiritual such as one might feel who is solitary on a lost planet. He flung himself on the heather and, with face buried in his arms shutting out the world, he began to think about himself. He lay there for hours, and when he rose to journey homewards the setting sun was reddening the battlement of the rocks and the valleys were brimming up with purple shadow. He walked on and on over the ridges and at last came to a cottage in the mountainside. As he entered he flung off the sadness which had beset him and spoke sweetly to the elders he called grandfather and grandmother. He ate the porridge and milk the old woman gave to him, and talked about the sea and the artist who was painting the mountain, but did not speak of the shining figure he had called the Shepherd of the Starry Flocks. He knew, though he was loved, that they looked doubtfully at times upon this child of their child, and that they wondered often if he was indeed a changeling as the people of the hills said of him. He knew this, for he could see their thoughts as he could feel their love. He went out after that and ran about the fields with other children, racing and shouting with them until voices from distant cottages began to call them home, and he too went back to the cottage where he lived, and, climbing a ladder, went into a little room where his bed lay close to a window looking across the valley and lake. Beyond that was the same great mountain which he had watched with the artist in the morning. He took up a fiddle which lay on a box and he began in the dark to play a melody of his own imagining. In the room below the old man, drowsing by a turf fire, heard the music and it awakened long-sleeping emotions. His heart was melted as when he was young, and he sat with wet eyes listening until the music ceased and there came a creaking which showed the boy had climbed into his bed.

It may have been an hour or hours may have passed. Aodh sat up in his bed. He looked through the open window. He saw the great mountain beyond the dark valley and the lake, but now it was crested with a glowing light like that he had seen in Paul's imagination. The boy's eyes were starry in the dark. The light beckoned him to it. He must go. In a moment he was out in the night and was hastening down the valley. He felt tireless and full of power as if he had not already roamed for many miles. The rocks glimmered greyly in the summer night. He leaped them more lightly than he had leaped them in the dawn.

Then he left the rocky fields behind and entered the black woods silvered here and there by flakes of moonfire. His feet moved as surely through the mazes of the blackness as through the light, and at last he came to the reed-fringed margin of the lake. He thought he saw silvery forms looking at him from the water but heeded them not. He strode along swiftly by the lake to its eastern shore, where he turned and entered anew the blackness of the woods which covered the mountain to its knees. The boy climbed upwards. He felt the huge mountain to be living. It poured its strength into him. There was a vibration in the air like that melody of the aether which had sounded on his ear, but now it grew until the mountain seemed mad with song. As he climbed from the last trees he saw far above him the light brightening on the highest plateau, and he ran up the steep side in his eagerness lest it might fade before he came. There were voices mingling with the music, voices ethereal and divinely gentle, yet with all the power of that great tone out of which they rose. As he overcame the last steep rock and stood on the turf of the plateau his eyes were dazzled, for there rose into the blue night a mighty and many-coloured palace, its pillars, walls and towers all luminous opal enwrought with precious fires and carven over with mythic forms. From the great gate came a blinding light, but the boy unterrified passed through it; and he was in the lofty hall and, through a light intense but clear, he saw many immortals shining as that figure he had beheld in dream, but beyond his dream in majesty, each on their thrones, with calm faces turned to him. As the child strode into the hall, the immortals from their thrones descending stood with bowed heads, for the child who was there was one of themselves, one who had left the Imperishable Light, laying aside sceptre and diadem and had narrowed himself to that body that he might waken the souls in the abyss of earth. At that moment Aodh was divested of the childhood into which he had imagined himself, and he towered up to a consciousness unimaginable and not to be fully remembered by his mortality, for it enveloped Earth and Heaven. He was struggling, when he wakened at dawn in his room, to recapture a lost magnificence of power. Had he been singing a song which went in every direction and into thousands of hearts? Had he blown shining images into myriads of darkened souls? Had he taken these from eternity to scatter the fiery seed through humanity? Or was the fiery seed already sown and did he but blow it to a vivid flame? The child mind was bewildered, and it was long before Aodh came to a surety about himself, for even the immortals when they put on mortality are but a little part of themselves, a spark in the immensity of their own fiery being.

VII

MEN are never nearer to the gods or more partakers of their ecstasy than when they are creators. Paul, incessantly creative, was the happiest of men. Seated in a glade of the forest he could see the branches, green-burdened and wind-swayed, make fire and darkness to reel to and fro on the russet floor. He watched the flying of tattered flame and purple shadow; and the mad dance of colour evoked whirling figures which rushed out of the house of the soul to mix with the reeling light. He could see swirling draperies, flushed faces, loosened and rippling hair, the glint of a white arm, a gleaming neck, the dance of lovely feet, all sun-flecked, dazzling and bewildering as the anarchy of flame and darkness in which they rioted. His heart was singing as his brush moved swiftly. If we were many-armed as an Indian god, he thought, one might keep pace with imagination. But the phantasmal figures went on dancing, being gay of themselves with a life of their own, and they would not be stayed in any one movement however beautiful. He pretended unhappiness, but all the while was delighted at his own swift mastery in evolving rhythm from chaos. So swiftly did his brush move that he surprised his hand shaping form ere an image had become present to consciousness. And suddenly he knew that the daimon, which had let loose the whirling figures, had also liberated energies which played on the strings of the body, directing hand and mind; and, if the mind wavered for a moment, the guidance of the hand was sure. For an instant he rose above himself and became one with that creative genius which is behind all conscious motion of the mind. He felt in that instant his being was rooted in some paradise of fiery and beautiful forms, ready to rush out through any open door to populate earth with their ecstatic life. Where did it all come from? Had there been a dance like that in some forest of antiquity with only the Eternal Mind to remember its beauty, and was it from that treasure-house the flock of images escaped? He went on painting, intoxicated with the beauty he saw and the beauty he imagined. The forest depths before him were a dazzle of green and sparry scintillations. Branches were suddenly burnished with vivid colour as suddenly vanishing.

Patches of orange flame awoke, blazed on the russet floor, then darkened to purple. There was incessant birth and death of light. Through it all went the dance of lovely shapes. Then into the figures of imagination a living figure raced, a girl running down the glade, the sunlight on her blue dress flecking it with a glow rich as the bloom on a peacock's tail. It was Conaire's child. She slipped behind him to look at the picture.

"Oh, Paul, how lovely! I want to dance! I want to dance!" and she went whirling about, face, flickering hair and dress fretted with light like the figures of his dream. At last she flung herself down on the moss beside him.

"Why isn't Aoife here to dance with me? She is like a daffodil in the sun—all burning."

"Who is this wonderful Aoife?"

"Aoife! The mountain, the lake and the woods as far as you can see are hers. I call her the Princess, because though she is only my age everybody has to be her servant."

"Must an old woman of twelve even be her slave?"

"Oh, Paul, I can't help it. I think she gets inside me, and can run in and out of me as if I was a cave. She sets me on fire."

"She keeps you to do her mischief for her as another young person keeps me!"

"No. It is not like that," said the child mysteriously. "She is like someone in the fairy tales. I never told anybody but you. I hear music inside the rocks when she is with me. Sometimes there are people like twinkling mists who come out of the mountain to look at her. And tall silvery people grow from the trees, gleaming people with long purple hair. I was frightened when I saw them, but Aoife laughed and clapped her hands, and they all faded back into the trees."

"You and your Aoife are living in fairyland now, sweetheart. And to think they are sending you both out of fairyland to Europe where never a dryad has been seen for thousands of years! Why are they doing it?"

"Father and mother think I ought to learn languages where they are spoken."

"Oh, Olive dear, don't let them take all the fairy out of your mind. If you do, the hills, when you come back, will be only rocks empty of music, and the bark door of the trees will be shut so that not a dryad can slip through to play with you."

"It is cruel of you even to think that. Why

should I grow out of seeing things any more than you?"

She sat looking at him reproachfully, the child's lovely face a pure oval, the eyes a rich grey with a spark of silver like a little star dancing in each, the fair hair falling in curves and clusters; and all of such beauty that Paul, gazing on her, lapsed into one of those mystical moods which what was beautiful more and more evoked in him. And she was no longer Conaire's child, but a fragile exquisite imagination of the Master of all arts who dreamed and devised it within and without, and held it together, face, eyes, innumerable hair, heart beating adorably, breathing body, grace of limb, through every motion, speaking through it to him, evolving it until it became the perfect mirror of the immortal thought in the immortal mind and could be a dwelling-place for the gentleness in that majesty. He murmured in his heart over this little citizen of the mystic empire, "Oh, if you should ever become an exile!" And a wild protest burned in him because the great Artist seemed to set out his masterpieces carelessly and without defence, so that miracles of beauty might be marred, and the lamp set within them be dimmed. And then something within him cried, "No! no! The Master never fails in His art. Through life, and through death to life again, He follows His works, and He will not cease until He has fashioned in immortal substance what was but evanescent air." He shook off his sadness and said gaily:

"No! You will never be out of hail of fairyland! Never! Yet it is tragic this going away to-morrow. But I'll steal you all for myself now, and we will row on the lake, and come to our own enchanted island, and light a fire there, and signal to the stars when they come out, and I'll have a whole afternoon of my dearest to remember when she is away."

He had been folding easel, gathering up brushes, paints and canvas; and with the child moving happily beside him he walked down the glade, and crossed a rushy field to a wooded promontory running out into the lake. His own cottage was there, built a little way from the trees. He cried to his elderly housekeeper: "Margaret. I want tea and a kettle full of water and a boat-load of cakes, for we are going to be wrecked on a desert island, and the earth will have to race a million miles from where it is before we get back."

He rowed out leisurely into the haze of sunny mist which lay on the lake, half rowing, half drifting, to a wooded island from which great branches stretched far out, sheltering lustrous shallows and inlets. It was a place in which he often sought solitude, and the mood of the Earth became life for him as he rested there, and the vision of the Earth was speech and no other speech was needed. They lay on the mosses, sometimes watching through half-closed eyes the roof of sunlit leaves quivering as if millions of emerald, blue and yellow birds were fluttering above them, sometimes watching the diamond dance of lights on the water. The lake, as the long afternoon ended, was burnished with gold and that melted into every iridescence. Paul with a half-sigh woke out of his dream, and then there was a bustle for fallen branches. The fire was lit, the kettle was boiled, the feast was spread. He invented many fantasies for their common delight. The isle became movable as the carpet of the magicians of Arabia, and he brought it to Eastern seas, or planted it as an oasis beside the ruins of great cities, and they had imaginary adventures with dusky races, and both agreed that when they died the island must go with them to Paradise. At last, looking through the leaves, Paul saw the Evening Star sparkling above the cliffs, and he said sadly, "Our day is over." They went to the boat and he rowed it back silently to the shore. The child stood looking at him when they landed. He saw her eyes were wet. She took his hand, pressed it to her wet cheek, and then ran away as if she could not bear a longer parting. He followed the little figure with his eyes until it was swallowed up in the darkening twilight. Over the hills the stars were moving in the paths appointed them, and it seemed that she, no less than the other stars, was guided on her way by the Great Shepherd.

VIII

"How great a hollow in life can be made by the absence of a very small person," said Conaire unhappily. He had come to Paul's cottage a month or two later. He moved restlessly about the room. "The flame of a candle is a minute thing. But when it goes out, what a great darkness there is!"

"Why did you let Olive go so far away?" asked Paul.

"Truly I do not know. I think some magic constrained me. There is a young girl a little older than Olive who will be a great lady, for hers are the forests, lakes and mountains all about us. When she first saw Olive some years ago she took possession of her as a young queen might, and Olive seems to belong to her more truly than to me or her mother. She is a beautiful quivering fire, this young Aoife. When I wanted Olive to remain here she blazed at me. I felt as if an indignant goddess was shrivelling me with lightning, and I was like some old half-wit who had halted a procession of princes. They have gone to a very rare and distinguished school. I could not myself afford this for Olive. But the guardians of that young Aoife—who ought rather to be called her slaves, for they are obedient to her whims as the genii to Aladdin and his lamp—when told she would not move unless Olive went with her, in their lordly way insisted that payment was their duty as they existed only for the happiness of their young despot. Do you know, Paul, if your vision of the warriors of heaven had been about a great house and not a cottage, I might have thought the Avatar to come was a goddess and that this wonder child was she. Well, while Olive is away I must try to find other lights to illuminate my darkness. Let us talk of that child we imagined as Avatar. The thought of him is often in my mind."

"He is often in my mind," said Paul. "Come, I will show you something"; and he left the cottage and walked through the woods until he came to a glade where was his studio, a building of wood all white with white pillars about it like a Greek temple. Conaire followed him within. The artist took two pictures and a drawing in coloured chalks and set them side by side on a ledge. The first was that cottage aureoled with light with its divine guardians holding their swords of wavering flame. The second was that dark mountain he had painted with its dragon crest of fire. The third was a pastel of the head of the boy who had been with him on the hill. It was a face full of light, a blue sky behind the head making the gold of his hair like curling flames.

"These three," he said, "have come, I hardly know why, to be connected together in my mind." He told Conaire about the boy who spoke to him for so few moments and passed lightly leaping up the hill. Conaire's eyes lit with excitement.

"Did you never think to trace the boy?"

"I did indeed, for his image had begun more and more to glow in my imagination. But when I thought of seeking him out in that countryside to which he was going I felt as if a constraining will was laid upon mine, and I was not to unveil the mystery of that boy. In his own time he will reveal himself, and he is not to be revealed by another. Oh, I have thought about him, and," he said hesitantly, as if he was half ashamed to be so impressed by the transient vision of a peasant boy, "I had a dream in which he came to a palace of the gods, and they stood bowed before him. "I do not know why it is, but the image of that boy darkens everything else in my imagination."

"And that dark flame-fringed mountain?" asked his friend. "What are your thoughts about that?"

"I do not know what I think. I hardly felt it was my own fingers guided the brushes, and it has haunted me ever since—that mountain. I look at it as some ancient might have looked at Mount Olympus or the fabulous Meru. I imagine a gate to the secret of the world in its heart. I find myself thinking of what may be hidden in it before I sleep, and when I waken sometimes I have the sense that I have been there with shining companions."

Then the elder began to conjure up out of memory or fantastic imagination a mysterious wisdom about the earth and its sacred places.

"To the ancients," he said, "Earth was a living being. We who walk upon it know no more of the magnificence within it than a gnat lighting on the head of Dante might know of the furnace of passion and imagination beneath. Not only was Earth a living being having soul and spirit as well as body, but it was a household wherein were god folk as well as the whole tribe of elemental or fairy lives. The soul of Earth is our lost Eden. This was the Ildathach or Many-coloured Land of our ancestors, and of which Socrates too spoke, saying Earth was not at all what the geographers supposed it to be, and there was a divine earth superior to this with temples where the gods do truly dwell. Our souls put on coats of skin. That is, they were lost in our bodies here, and at last we fell together outside the divine circle and came to live on surfaces, not even dreaming that within the earth is a spirit which towers up within itself from clay and rock to the infinite glory. Only the poets and mystics have still some vision of the lost Eden. The gods are still in the divine household, and the radiance over the palaces of light appear at times to seers like yourself as dragon-crests of flame or rivers of light running out to the stars. It is time for us to be travelling inward, and, if there be an Avatar to come, he may show us the way once more as did the Avatars of the past. How do I know all this? The Earth Spirit has been talking to me ever since I came here, telling me the meanings of all I have read and many things which never were written, and it confirmed that dream I told you about, that there would come a day when the immortals once more would walk among us and be visible heroes to us."

Paul looked affectionately at his old friend to whom the universe was such a romance, and he would have asked a question which, he knew, would have started Conaire on a monologue of an hour, when there was a sound of footsteps behind him. He turned and saw a slight figure with a beautiful elfish face, who walked as if his body was charged with energy. It was another friend, Felim Carew, the poet, who began at once with a tempest of friendly denunciation.

"I have found you out at last—you who denounced the money kings for their monstrous greed. But their sin was innocence compared with yours. They only kept money for themselves, a thing which is not worth keeping. I do not grudge it to them any more than I grudge straws and feathers to a madman. But you discovered here a world of unfallen beauty, beauty for which we starved, and you kept the beauty to yourself. I am going to write an epic like Dante and put you in the lowest hell, face to face with Satan's masterpiece of ugliness. It will be a punishment for your silent greed in keeping to yourself the loveliest country on earth. Is it any wonder you paint pictures which people fall over each other to possess when you have not even to exercise imagination? You have only to pick up the loveliness which lies all about you while we have to sweat blood to make a thing of beauty. Oh, but that is wonderful!" His quick eyes had been roaming about while he talked, and he had seen the aureoled cottage with its divine watchers. "You must tell me about that! It is you have become the poet. But I have broken in between you and your friend!"

"No," said Conaire. "You only continue what we were speaking of, the mystery and magnificence of this mountainous nature. Earth, I see, has accepted you, for she inspires you to continue our conversation." He looked with great friendliness on the new-comer. Each had heard the artist speak of the other and they at once slipped into what seemed an old intimacy.

"I walked my way up here. I knew I had come into a country which was still in the divine keeping. I was on a hillside last evening and I watched girls and children lighting a fire. And I swear to you, Paul, there was some master of their souls and bodies who lived within them all and made every motion rhythmical and beautiful, as if a greater than Phidias had invented the harmony of their movements with each other, with clouds, blown boughs and the quivering waters of a stream. For three marvellous moments the invisible artist made masterpiece after masterpiece, and then, as if he had run to other souls to make another wonder, the rhythm was broken, and the children parted as leaves might fall from a withering blossom. Your eyes should have seen it. How could I put that visible magic into poetry! But you are not going to keep this enchanted land to yourself. I'll make it famous. No, I won't. You are right to be reticent. The earth will call to it all whom it thinks worthy. I am going to write better poetry than anyone, for I will wrestle with earth and will not let it go until it blesses me."

"Shall we initiate him into the mysteries?" the artist asked Conaire.

"Let him brood on the pictures, and if he is to be initiated it will appear from his interpretation."

The poet looked at the three pictures, and, after a silence of some moments, he turned to the others.

"A divine child! A manger, heavenly guarded! A holy mountain!"

"He is accepted," said Conaire, and the three talked late into the night.

IX

THE poet, who had neither dream nor vision to build on, was strangely the most earnest in faith that the darkness of earth was to be invaded from the heavens, and yet he would not have any search made for the Avatar.

"He will reveal himself in his own time. Though as yet he may be only a boy he may be doing his work. He may be like that Cuchulain of the Irish hero tales of whom it was said, 'This man protects Ireland more when he sleeps than when he wakes!' Do we know what happens when we sleep and pass beyond dream? We do not know what we do. We do not know what an avatar may do when his body is still. He may narrow himself here into the being of a child. But is he narrowed in that other world beyond dream—the world of spirit waking? Your visions and imaginations and the imaginations of others may be fiery arrows shot by a being all light. I may be here because I am called. I think I am. I was for a year in that New World of marvellous cities. Nothing that the most fantastic imagination dreamed of Babylon or Nineveh comes near the reality of these gigantic heaven-assailing cities. You stand in the heart of one and look up from the gloom of the street, and a thousand feet or more above you the sunlight blazes on great towers and terraces. There may be a dazzle of flame where burnished plates of metal, silvery or bronze, catch fire from the sun and burn like giant candles. There are tall towers all a glitter of glass. And, oh, the wonder at night! There are lights faint as stars on the topmost storeys, and the stars themselves seem but the continuation of a fabulous architecture reaching up to infinity. These cities are the last trap set for the spirit of man to draw him from nature and from himself. The people who live in them are kind, but, oh, so unhappy. They fly from one sensation to another and the way from body to soul is lost. If they close their eyes they are in a darkness which frightens them. They cannot bear to be still or alone. They are thirsty for beauty but cannot create it within themselves. When they meet a soul, truly living, natural and prodigal in itself, they are filled with wonder. They try to express their reverence by filling up every moment for it with the sensations which have atrophied their own imaginations. Ninety per cent of their people live in these unimaginable cities which they began lifting to the clouds three hundred years ago when the race was in its childhood. They created out of an abundant physical energy a prodigious mechanism which goes on swelling out of its own inherent vitality, building and organising, until the mechanism has overwhelmed life. They cannot help themselves, poor people. They were born into the mechanistic maze and do not know the way out. There was never anything in the world so pitiful as their souls. They are rich inconceivably without, but paupers within, supplicating alms from any stray genius. They have become alien to nature, the ancient Mother. In its silences and lonelinesses they might meet the outcast majesty of spirit; and to the poor soul that outcast majesty would be a thing of terror. They would not recognise it as themselves. How could they be saved? If I was dictator I would take them in hundreds of thousands, and chain each one as a solitary to a stone in the desert or to a rock in the hills, give them a blanket or two and a little food. I would chain them to the rock as Prometheus was chained, and let the infinite heavens, sun, moon, stars and wind, be tormentors in their solitude until they had made friends with sky, sun, stars, moon, wind and earth, and they found in the anger of the gods there was a love; until the silences became friendly and the hollows of air no longer a void, and the stones were sweet to the touch. I cast all my thoughts about this on the air to a hundred million listeners and then flew over here to know what you were doing. It is enchanted, this western land of yours, not for its mountains, not for lake, river and heath, but because it seems alive. And, Paul, there are the strangest folk here, drawn, as I think I was and you were, by that mystic nature. I walked day after day and felt the mountains were swallowing me up. It is not the poet you knew who is here, but the Earth Spirit who sits and prattles by your hearth. Make the most of it while it is with me for it may leave me, though I will never leave it, but will pursue it and cry to it as Jacob to the angel, 'I will not let you go until you bless me.' "

Paul and Conaire sat listening, pleased by the fantasy of the poet, and, as Paul looked at the elfish figure, it seemed to his imagination to be enveloped in a dark blue shining air, transparent as the blue of night, and there seemed innumerable sparks flashing like gold in that dark purity of blueness.

"Even the ruins of humanity here," the poet went on, "have some wild poetry in them. I was walking on a mountain road the day before yesterday and an old man came along, the remains of a magnificent human being, with a ruined beauty on his face. The old man was hugging his body to himself with his arms, shaking and swaying in his grief. And his sorrow was so great that he must speak it, even if it was only to another vagabond like himself. He stayed me and said, 'Over those hills I wandered forty years ago. Nobody but myself knows what happened under the thorn tree forty years ago. The fret is on me! The fret is on me! God speaks out of His darkness, "I have and I have not. I possess the heavens. I do not possess the world." Abroad if you meet a countryman he will give you the bit and the sup. But if you come back to your own country after forty years it is not the potato and bit of salt you get, but only "Who's that ould fellow?" The fret is on me! The fret is on me!' Was the old man drawn back at the end of his days to remember a young beauty? 'Nobody knows but myself what happened under the thorn tree forty years ago!' Will that remembered beauty be the candle which will light him into Paradise? Oh, they are strange these mountain folk! What wisdom is born in their silences! I found a boy tending sheep a hundred miles from this, and he was staring at the sky and I asked him what he thought, and he said: 'I am thinking we once lived in the Sun.' But he had no words to tell of the great glory he had imagined. I found an old woman listening to a music coming out of the hills. She was muttering to herself 'They are singing there. They are dancing there to-night,' and I tell you, Paul, I heard a faint tinkling coming out of a ridge of rock as of innumerable elf creatures playing on I know not what magical instruments. Besides these folk whose minds have been shaped for centuries by the earth they lived on, there are many refugees from cities as you are. The masters of the world who organised production and found that wheat could be grown here and fruit there, and cattle fattened most economically in other places, left out of their calculations these mountainy places where there could be no cheap mass production. But, neglecting these, they made it possible for rebels against the mechanical to live there, people who can, by the produce of two or three acres, feed themselves and escape slavery. There are odd groups of workers in arts and crafts, little colonies of earth lovers. There is a dark, fierce, fantastical man you must know. His name is Gregor. There is a sculptor and his wife I met. There are obscure mystics scattered about everywhere. I never met such adorable wild people. They all seem to have woven into them some tapestry of nature and their being is shot through and through with threads of light. They are the nucleus of an army in conflict with the vast mechanism of the world. They are mobilising the great silences, mountains, lakes, sun and wind; things that have no hands to smite, making ready for the last battle between light and darkness. They will make themselves invincible by these gentle eternal things, and, by God, they will win even if the battle should last ten thousand years. This country of stones the masters of the world neglected. It is there the temple of the future will be built."

Paul and Conaire had the delight men have who listen to praise of their best-beloved. Then the poet began again:

"I am not going to leave this country. I will tramp about it until I find the place where earth is most friendly to me and will sing to me most. I am going to be lazy," he said with a whimsical smile, "and let the Earth Spirit make my songs for me as it makes your pictures for you. I saw lovely things of yours in the galleries. But," his restless eyes had been looking about the studio, "you keep the masterpieces for yourself."

"Yes," said Paul, "all of a certain character I keep. I do not like parting from them. They seem to belong to each other and throw a reflected light from picture to picture."

"Yes, I see that. It is a new realm of nature you are revealing. They connect with each other as we do. We are like planets drawn to circle about an invisible sun. The only thing of interest about us now is what reflected lights may shine on us from whatever divinity is to be the new lamp of the world."

X

It was Midsummer Eve. A fairy stillness was in the air. The only glow came from that girdle of green fire which all night long lay about the earth in midsummer nights. Paul and the poet sat on a hillock looking over tide-deserted sands to a long black ridge lying like some monstrous animal half on earth and half crouched in water. There were apparitions like silver stars that glowed and went out and glowed again and ran along the blackness of the ridge.

"See, the lights of fairy!" whispered Paul. "They hold festival to-night. It is Midsummer Eve. Do you see? Below there on the sands! Those tall flame-coloured people who move in some mystic ritual!"

"How lovely! How wonderful! Their dance seems to be god-guided. Are they those who never fall out of Eden? They move all with the innocence of unfallen life. Are we to go back to their world?"

"No. These are only the slaves of light. That life lies far behind us. We, I think, shall go back to a brighter light than that which opened up the story of the cycles."

"Something is going to happen, Paul. What is it? Is a new religion to be born? What magic will it exercise over us? I hope it will be the magic of the Gay. Are they not terrible in their sadness these religions of the Iron Age? The Light is never hailed with joy. 'The Light shineth in the darkness and the darkness comprehendeth it not.' 'He came to His own and His own received Him not.' The mystery is told in tears as if we must understand sorrow better than joy. The real betrayal of Jesus was not by Judas but by the other apostles who would not speak of the laughter of Jesus, He who went to feastings and merriments, gay at heart as all must be who know their immortality. I pine for something gay and beautiful. I swear to you, Paul, I want to wear cap and bells before the Throne, to clash cymbals and dance, not abase myself before the Lord with my nose in the dust and my hinder parts pointed to the heavens like crawling saints in the religious pictures."

They both broke into laughter. The spell of the fairy stillness was broken. They rose and went their ways, the poet to Conaire whose guest he was. "I love that old man," he said.

Paul went his own way, but after his lively companion had departed, the spell of Midsummer Night—the most enchanted night in the year, when the barriers between this world and that other are fragile—fell on him again. There was a wild restlessness in body and soul. Imaginations crowded on him. His feet, unconsciously to himself, began to move swiftly, driven by an energy born in the psyche. He drew nigh his cottage but turned away again and strode across the dark miles of sand. He walked like one pursued not by terrifying but by noble furies who pelted him with celestial fire. He was overwhelmed. His body was unable to bear the hurricane of power; and at last, below that long black ridge of rock, half fainting, he sat down on a stone and buried his head upon his knees. As he sat there he became more still. The horizon of soul seemed to widen, to spread far beyond the body to a distant light. Whether it rushed at him or whether he was borne to it he could not afterwards say. But in imagination he was buoyed up on some shining aether which welled, a dazzling fountain, from the heart of earth. Where the fountain broke out of Anima Mundi in the blinding centre he saw the likeness of a being white as the sunfire. What was that being? A celestial singer? A heavenly poet? A magician of the beautiful? From it poured dazzling images and forms of ethereal loveliness. It was that being that had blown on him with fiery breath. From it came that hurricane of imaginations. The light illuminated earth and its children from within. It searched out every heart. It came with a burning message to those who seemed to wear the colour of truth. Paul remembered ancient legends of his country of a Fountain which flowed invisibly bathing the soul. He was wondering what god had unsealed the fountain, and then the fierce illumination faded. But, before it departed, eyes that seemed to have looked only on eternity looked into his own, and he was awed as if omniscience was pondering upon him. With its fading came the face of a child, and then he was back in himself and was seated on his stone alone in the night looking over the desert miles of sand. He sat there long and long, and at last went homeward, filled with a spiritual exaltation. He knew the tongues of fire with which he had been baptized would be wisdom in him, and the will of the power would be seen in the work of his hands.

XI

The day following that midsummer night was heavenly still and clear. A pure and silver glory pervaded the blue air. The clouds on far horizons bowed low like young awed cherubim. The waters in the lake hardly stirred, parting their lips as if to sing but were silent, breathing only joy deep in each other. Everything, light, water, air, cloud and rocky earth, seemed to belong to an unfallen nature. Paul himself, the last night's tumult of vision and imagination stilled, felt ethereally light within. He might have been one of the earth's unfallen children ere Eden was clouded from our eyes. He sat as in a trance gazing on a nature that seemed living from earth to utmost distances of sky. It was gazing at him, that living nature, as he was gazing into it. The magical fingers of air and light made music in his being, playing as on a lute strung by Heaven. How had man lost that vision of infinite life? What had they thought precious enough to turn them from the endless wonders created by the mighty artist who at his feet made the melody of the flowers, each a miracle of art, wild rose, orchid, honeysuckle, fern. If they had been dilated to the immensity of space they would still have been flawless. There were depths within these marvellous depths, worlds within worlds, and heavens beyond the heaven of heavens, each with its divine populace. The majesty which held constellations and galaxies, suns, stars and moons inflexibly in their paths, could yet throw itself into infinite, minute and delicate forms of loveliness with no less joy, and he knew that the tiny grass might whisper its love to an omnipotence that was tender towards it. What he had felt was but an infinitesimal part of that glory. There was no end to it.

There was a rustle of feet in the grass behind him. He turned and saw Carew, who came and sat down beside him and lay there in a long silence. Some magic had stilled for a while the restless flame of his mind, and it was only after an hour had passed that he began to speak, dreamily.

"I think the Golden Age has returned. Everything one imagined seems possible. This day is the forgiveness of sins, and when the God forgives there is no withholding of love. Everything is as it was on the first day.

We are made virginal and receive once more the primal blessings of ecstasy and beauty. If one of the gods leaned out of that hollow air now and said, 'Felim, come with me,' I would take his hand and climb up the airy way to his home, and think it only natural that we should be friends, his greatness and my littleness. I would sing him my songs and he would make wonders for me by his art. Paul, there must be some way of getting out of the body. While I was lying here I asked myself why were we prisoners. Why are we so tied to grass and stones—tied to ourselves still more? I am like a thief pent in solitary confinement in a cell. I am packed round with thick clay and bound to the bone. Outside I can see what treasures there are, what galleys laden with stars sail to unknown beaches. How rich the Kingdom must be when the King can scatter his jewels so prodigally on moths and butterflies! If I could get out of my cell, the psyche would have wings for far flights. What a universe there would be to loot if we were out of our cells! If the Lord hears me talking He will know what to expect if I break prison." He laughed. "Oh, I am so happy to-day I could clap my hands and dance. But no, I must not. I feel tender to everything living.

See, I lift my feet from the ground lest I hurt my fellow-prisoners, grass and flowers. O little pimpernel, who stare up at me so gallantly, do not fear me. I am no ogre. I am only a little looser on my legs than you are. You too, little ruddy star, will get free. It may be aeons away, but assuredly you will get free, and you will mount so high that you will glow on air, a burning blossom, looking down on earth below, and its people will fold their palms and adore you. Everything, little pimpernel, is hurrying godwards, and you will get there, changing from flower to star on the way. You believe that, Paul?"

"Yes, I believe everything you say."

"And why not? The atom is always trembling into the infinite in our imagination, and it is right, for the atoms are the creation of the infinite and they bear signs of that majestic ancestry. The final gift of the infinite to its children will be itself. I am prodigal of intuitions to-day. Is there not something different in earth as if it had wakened from long sleep, its soul had come back to its body. And now it has wakened, its body is flushed with magical life. That is not the water of yesterday, nor the air, nor the earth. Some heavenly wine is mixed with the water, and in the air we breathe there is a mingling of the Holy Breath. Earth is living under our feet. It was in a world like this ages ago all the mythologies and fairy tales were born. And they were all true, true to something in our own being. Once more there can be natural spirituality. I went out early this morning and I was reborn. Why do we ever sleep at the hour of miracles? I made then this song, or it made itself for me:

"O, dark holy magic,
To steal out at dawn,
To dip face and feet in grasses
The dew trembles on,
Ere its might of spirit healing
Be broken by the dawn.

"O, to reel drunken
On the heady dew;
To know again the virgin wonder
That boyhood knew;
While words run to music, giving voices
To the voiceless dew.

"They will make, those dawn-wandering
Lights and airs,
The bowed worshipping spirit
To shine like theirs.
They will give to thy lips an aeolian
Music like theirs.

"That natural spirituality is growing around us in the folk we meet. Conaire has natural spirituality. So have you. It is in many others and you must meet them, Paul. You are becoming a hermit with only mountains and stones for companions. They are good company. But I want you to give up this afternoon and night to me and come for a tramp. You shall choose your own way. Spiritual gravitation will bring us to our kinsmen, or if it brings us only to other hills, then these are our kinsmen also. There are adorable people living about among these mountains whom you would love. It is as easy to walk in and out of their minds as if you had known them for a million years. I feel so certain you must meet some of these spiritual kinsmen that I will not show you the way. They may not be better company than the stones of the field with which you are in league. But they know you are there and they will talk to you and are as transparent as crystal. I called them by their Christian names when I met them first. It is delightful to speak by their intimate names to friends without knowing what other names they have."

XII

"I WILL take, then, the hill road southward," said Paul. "It is easier to walk on the high ridges than on the level road."

"Yes, I found that. It must have been on a hill-top that Antaeus wrestled with Hercules. It is on the hills the Earth Spirit puts fire into one's feet every time we touch her. Is it that earth breath you painted in serrations of flame about the sacred mountain?"

"That was a vision. I only know after a while when I lie on the hillside with closed eyes that the dusk disappears under my eyelids. I see waves of brilliant colour. Never is imagination so vivid. The barrier between worlds is fragile there and one can peer from this world to that as through a transparency."

All roads are easy to the traveller with whom imagination is a companion. The leagues dwindle to furlongs and the mountains to mounds. After a time they paused at the highest point of the ridge. The artist lay back on the heather, while his friend wandered about. Paul looked up into blue deeps of air. Like those seers before whose gaze, concentrated on a crystal, visionary forms appear, he had found his magic mirrors for vision in deep pools of water and the vaster ocean of air. Gazing into the first mirror of water he had passed through it into lustrous worlds which lay within the being of earth; and often looking into that other mirror of cloudless blue he had seen its depths stained with brilliant colour: palaces glowing with amethyst, gold and every hue of the rainbow, and there moved the cloud-brilliant populace of sky. One mirage of remote beauty after another had enchanted his eyes fixed on that mirror. Gradually he lost himself in those depths. He heard faintly the footsteps of his friend who moved about, and at last, half in a dream, he heard the voice of the poet. He looked round. Carew with shut eyes was standing beside him, his hands groping as if to touch some invisible thing. The poet's voice came to him wholly out of his dream.

"I feel blown by an invisible wind inward. Though I am steady on my legs I tell you I am dream-tipsy. I have been tossed between moon and sun and stars and visions of water, wind, hills and forests. They come to me as ancient intimates. I had known them millions of years ago. They were once within me. We parted from ourselves, I know not how or why. We have played hide-and-seek with each other through the aeons. And now they come near. The spirit in them is as near to me as the beatings of my own heart. Now we meet again it is like the meeting of lovers who had parted but yesterday. The immortals never forget their loves through all inbreathings and out-breathings of the universe. Come with me, Paul. There is endless wonderful travelling here. There are divine transfigurations that await us. We will be changed inconceivably as we go on. I am changed within myself. My feet here are tied to stone and grass. But I, where am I? Am I treading the meadows of the sun? What are these burning blossoms that glow by their own light? Who are those about me who look as if they were consumed from within by love for some ineffable beauty? There is ecstasy under their closed eyelids. Their feet are god-guided as if they were dancers at the bridal of Love and Death."

As his companion spoke Paul almost came to community of vision with the poet. He saw lovely forms which seemed to emit light, and half saw the rapture of faces lit by the last ecstasy of surrender to a divinity which drew them into itself. The poet became silent, as if in his mystic travelling he had come to a being for whose remote wonder no words in human speech had any affinity. At last he came back to earth, his eyes blinking like one who has come out of a blazing room into the darkness of night.

"Where am I? How dark it is! How remote is everything! I am outcast from heaven. I was melting into divinity, and there came some flicker of earth into my soul, and I am here again. I am only a vagrant poet, and how little and tremulous is my song!"

"You see," said Paul, "as the poets ages ago saw into Ildathach, the many-coloured land. It was so Bran saw through this world the blossoms burning in some heavenly forest. I could follow you but a little. You went away from me. Another time we must try to see together."

They walked on silently, Paul leading the way into a country which was unknown to him. Earth had grown multicoloured. Through hazes of light the ridges glowed with pale gold. The hollows of the valleys were pools of blue and purple shade. At last they dropped to lower levels. Paul saw a house which even at a distance created a sense of beauty and fitness as if it was as natural an outcrop of earth as rocks or trees.

"It was an artist built that: I wonder who?"

"That was designed by Mark, the sculptor I spoke to you about. Mary his wife told me he sat for days looking at that recess within the hills until the image of the house arose before him. He says that is the form the stones there would have dreamed themselves into if they had dreams."

The door to it was open, and there was nobody in sight. The poet entered as if sure of welcome. He turned into a great room. There were many figures in clay. He pointed to some of these.

"Those are Mark's, and these," pointing to a multitude of little figures, "are done by the young folk about here. Mark teaches them to play with clay, while Mary inspires them to sing and dance and even to make songs for themselves. The making of figures is a delightful play to them. They never had thought of praise or profit. See how good this is in intention!"

He held up a little group of two girls leaning against a rock.

"Has it not a natural grace? Look at those weeders! What rhythm in their bent bodies!

And that dancer! Does she not seem as if she was foam tossed up from some invisible fountain?"

The artist was delighted with the play of the children. But his eyes were more drawn by the sculptor's own imaginations. He stood long before one figure whose whiteness rose out of stone as if it was earth-born. An uncouth animal shape was heaving its haunches out of clay with its forefeet straining against the earth for complete emancipation. And itself seemed to be changing; for, as in the centaur the human rises out of the animal, so from that monstrous earth-born creature rose a lovely winged figure with face cast upward as if it was beating its way into air. As the monster had struggled out of earth and rock so out of the brute the psyche was winging its way into the heavenly aether.

"That is genius," he said. Then he saw a relief. There were two airy figures flying wingless as if by their own volition. One was pointing exultantly earthwards where a skull lay. Over the relief was carven the words, "That was once thy dwelling-place." There was another mystical figure, Minerva rising from the head of a Jove with the vast blind face of an earth god. In all this mystic sculptor's work was the sense of transfiguration and escape. Paul would have lingered but Felim drew him outside. "Mark and Mary must be near by. Ah, there is Mary!"

A graceful dark-eyed girl a little way from the house sat between tree-roots leaning back against the trunk and looking over a valley now growing to a rich gloom.

"Mary, this is Paul."

The girl greeted the new-comer as if he was a pleasant thought of her own which had just come into her mind.

"You must not think it was I who brought him here." The poet insisted upon the philosophy of their coming. "It was the law of spiritual gravitation."

"It is a good law, Felim," said the girl.

"I was going to ask for Mark, but it seemed to show mistrust in the law."

"Here he comes," the girl smiled. "See the law guiding his feet!"

The sculptor greeted Paul with the same air of natural acquiescence in intimacy that his wife had. The poet assumed control over the gathering. His quickened imagination started him on a speculation over what they were doing.

"We have been in the studio. I see something there you do not see. You are rooted here as Paul is in his own place. It is I who have been the roamer over hundreds of miles of country. There are tribes of folk who are our spiritual kinsmen inspired to do just such things. There are potters and painters and poets of sorts like myself, drifted out of the suffocation of the cities. What I see is an identity of character and inspiration in all they and you are doing. It is the birth of a new culture. They are all tipsy with dream as indeed I am myself. It was so all the great cultures of the past began, not in great cities. They died in the cities. But they were born in remote country places, in mountain valleys and on hills, with whisperings and breathings out of a mysterious nature. There was a music made by some Master-Singer and all who were bathed by the music had to dance to the tune. That unity of mind you see in ancient civilisations is beginning here. Do not the arts in the Egypt of antiquity seem to us in retrospect to be the creation of one mighty mind, the moulder of generations. The least workman who decorated a mummy-case had something in him guiding his fingers, something that was akin to the solemn temple-builders and the carver of sphinx and statue. Is there not the same harmony with all its variety in the Grecian mind? So it was with Chinese, Chaldeans, Hindus and Mayas. I think the invisible player now is pulling out a new stop on his organ, and the music with a new note is quickening many spirits."

"I like to hear Felim talking," said the girl. "He is like a gilded herald running before a great king blowing a trumpet. But you are hungry men. After supper I want to hear all about the celestial musician."

"He is always telling me things I know already," said Mark, "though I did not know them until he had spoken. He makes me feel as if I was dark and blind with unrealised profundities."

"He is a disturber of slumber," said Mary. "I know I shall go to bed to-night with a thousand torches blazing under my eyelids. But I will forgive if he comes now and will talk after. He will turn our daily bread into the substance of fairy."

XIII

They sat later in the warm and friendly night. Beyond the valley a vast moon rose redly over dark hills.

"What a night! Heaven and Earth seem one being." Carew spoke dreamily.

"The universe is an everyday companion, Felim," the girl spoke. "But it is too silently wise. You are a rarer visitor and the gods gifted you with flowing speech. You were to talk to us about the Master-Singer and the new music to which we are to move."

"If you brood on what Mark is already doing and on what you yourself are doing, you have your answer. What is in the minds of the children who flock to you? What about those two delightful young people who tell you their dreams?"

"Ah, you remember Rory and Aileen! They are wonderful. I met them to-day, oh so proud and dignified. They spoke to me as if they were ancients of the earth, far older than I was. They had been reading a coloured history of Egypt, and discovered they had lived before, for old Egyptian men came living out of the book. There were temples and sphinxes hovering about them. A tall Egyptian rose out of Rory, while Aileen was changed to a dusky girl with black braided hair, and the boy and girl bowed to each other solemnly and said 'We meet again.' The rest of their day was a longing for that ancient home of theirs. They told me with wounded dignity, 'We'd go there if they'd let us. They never think when they call us children and send us to bed that we are old like that inside.' "

"How enchanting! What a romance their lives must be!"

"They go on marvellous adventures in their imagination. Their imagination is so vivid I think they do not know whether they lived them or only imagined them. They become all kinds of great people. Once they were air chiefs, not of boats like those which fly over our heads, but boats which blew themselves along. And in one of these boats they went back through a thousand ages and came to themselves as they were in old De Danann times. Once they dreamed themselves into the heart of a mountain, and they told me when they were there there was no mountain at all but a blaze of light like the sun within the world."

"It is out of such children the new world will be born," said Felim. "Are they not dancing to a new music, linking heaven and earth in their hearts? Out of these adventures and memories will come what age in the thought, what skill in the deed, what gaiety in the heart."

"I think myself," said the girl, "their dreaming began when the Fairy Fiddler first came here."

"Who is the Fairy Fiddler?"

"A peasant boy. A strange and most beautiful child. They call him a changeling and think he is not right in his head. He has never been to school. But he plays marvellously on his fiddle. I think he must be like the poet of the Kalevala:

> Winds and waters my instructor.

After I heard him I lay down and cried and cried, for he made me feel the happiness and heartache of infinite desire. I first saw him on a rock by the roadside, his long gold hair blown back by the wind. He was playing to some children and it was the loveliest sight, the boy-player, the whirling of colour, the rippling of hair and the twinkling of feet. When I would have spoken to him he was gone, and the children scattered, their dance broken like a flower that had tumbled into pieces. The boy roams by himself over the country. I believe he must be a changeling as they say, for when I close my eyes and think about him I seem to see fairy lights dancing about his head."

Felim's hand pressed Paul's in the dark.

"That must be your boy," he whispered.

"Do you not sometimes find," the girl went on, "that those you meet often create ideal images of themselves on the heart, and seem to be changing into light?"

"Why should they not when for every man on earth there is a Seraph in his beauty in the divine world! What we really love in others is not what they seem to the outer but to the inner vision. I believe," said the poet, catching fire from his own thought, "that the psyche holds in itself the most wonderful and indescribable forms in which it robes itself in its travelling through the spheres. I am sure, Mary, behind that mask of girlhood there is a nymph, a dryad, an oread, a goddess and I know not what other creatures. Perhaps there is an angel. There certainly is a pixie."

"There is, Felim," said the girl, laughing. "She is here now listening to a kinsman's voice."

"You think I am not serious! Come and look at Paul's pictures. He is a seer and he is painting the earth visible and invisible, all the shapes the soul takes in its travels from earth to sky."

"Yes, if we may, we would be happy, Mark and I."

"You will see how much kinship there is between his art and Paul's. They are players on different instruments but in the same new orchestration of life."

"I wish the music you imagine would draw our friend Gregor into its harmony. He haunts those who have faith yet he derides them. Yet there must be some deep fountain of faith in him, if, as you say, it is spiritual gravitation brings us together. I think that he is striding up the road. He must have sent a thought of himself before him."

"You must meet him, Paul," said Felim. "There is a kind of lofty, dark, exasperated nobility about him. He will attack us, but it will be out of a profundity of feeling which measures everything by its own depths. Is that Gregor?" he called out as a tall dark figure passed beneath them on the mountain road. "Come up. Here is Paul Heron I want you to meet."

The man he called climbed up to the grassy mound, lifted a hand vaguely in greeting to them all, then laid himself down beside them, silent at first as if he continued a reverie that had absorbed him before he was called. The poet, who had elements of subtle impishness in him, wished to rouse that dark exasperation of protest he had spoken of as characteristic. He dangled a provocative fancy before the new-comer.

"I always thought the Golden Age never really departed from earth. Driven out of cities and palaces it still lingers in remote valleys like this. I am now certain of this, because it has even cast its spell on Gregor."

"On a night like this you could almost impose your fancy on me. God knows I wish I could think with you people whom I love more than any in the world. I would be much happier. But it is all self-begotten fantasy this idealism of yours. It is like the flickering of light over immovable stone; or at highest, but mirrored majesties, the reflections many times reverberated of profundities in the universe, and no more real than reflections are. Truth must be a state of being, and must include in unity or identity of consciousness the vast masonry of this earth, the deeps of space, the stars that move so resistlessly, as well as flowers and grass and you and I. I love listening to you, but I keep touching the granite with my fingers to keep my sense of the profundity and strength of things."

"Is not imagination our best way to apprehend truth? Is not what you have just said an imagination no less than Felim's fantasy?"

"Whatever reality is on us must be in the will. It is only when we will we find something real in ourselves, when we find we can stay ourselves against the stream of things, against our thoughts which bewilder us, even against love. Our imaginations are unreal and come and go. Desires too have their flow and ebb. All are phantasmal. The will only is the self-moving. When it is keen and burnished like a star it may become kin with or slip into unity with the will that sustains all things. The ancients knew this. A seer in the Upanishads spoke of the hierarchy of human faculties, and, above poetry in speech, above thought, above imagination, mind, wisdom or understanding, he placed strength, and said, 'One strong man can make a thousand men of understanding tremble.' It is, he said, by strength the earth stands, the sky stands, the mountains stand and the divinities rule. So I try to nourish the will and send what fiery arrows may be in my quiver against that world order which keeps the will in abeyance."

"But are not the faculties a high companionship of equals in essentials rather than a hierarchy?" asked the artist, who himself gave first place to the creative imagination.

"It is possible we may rise to a state where the faculties in their perfection will be blended into a unity. But here only the exercise of the will makes us aware of a reality in ourselves. I am not able to sustain that unrelaxing intensity of will that I spoke of. I am susceptible to influences from people like yourselves. Nature too has her own magic and can melt me as indeed I was melted last night. You who are the naturally spiritual could not, I think, have known of the exquisite anguish of joy at an awakening of the spirit I felt, I who had lived for forty years in cities, and had never realised in the haste and brilliance of life without, that within, under closed eyelids, there was a midnight of black unalterable air: I did not suspect that inner darkness until my first coming to this country many years ago. I lay on the hillside and found a brilliance of colour under the sheltered sight and wondered at it. When I went back to the city it had gone. But I became filled with a passion to have this sweetness of light within me and so I returned here. It seems a frail beginning for what later brought about an avalanche in my life. It was first an aesthetic, but it was changed later into a spiritual impulse. How great a price we must pay to be made luminous within! Every desire, every thought, is either the opening or the closing of a door to that light. A passionate desire and there is an instant thickening of the walls. To bring about a resurrection I had to give up my place in the world, my ambition, my power, my mistresses, the riot of the senses, and at last I settled here, seeking for allies in the silences of the hills, in water, grass, stones, the sweet immortal things. But even here I can only sustain the soul from slipping back by a never-ceasing will. I realised that only when I willed was I real to myself, and that all else was fugitive and phantasmal. That is why I dare not surrender to the luxury of dream. I do not dare to travel your road. Yet indeed last night I was melted as I had never been melted before, and I was made partner in some marvellous sweetness in the universe. I had all your faith for an hour, and believed like a child that all the fairy tales might be true, and I might yet come to the Land of Promise—oh, I was just such another sweet fool as yourselves, and had a bitter time exorcising this frailty."

"But that was a great happiness, Michael," the girl said softly.

"Yes, but I do not know whether it was not the ancient sensuousness transfigured taking on a more exquisite form. If I had surrendered myself to it I might have been dream-betrayed into my old passions once more. There's many a lovely Paradise in Hell, you know. If we rest in them, the old dragons of lust rise again out of a sweet cheating of the senses. There can be for me only the way of the will. Now you know, dear people, why I am at war with the world, and why, though I love you and your ideas, I dare not admit them, for they might not be to me what they are to you, and the famished devil in me might take hold of them to deliver my soul once more into safe keeping of the body."

There was a journey of many miles before Paul and Felim could come to home and bed. They rose with regret. There were promises of further meetings as they said good-night to the others.

On their way homeward the poet said, "Did not spiritual gravitation bring you to your own kin? There are many like these you can meet in further travelling. And you will meet them." He said of Gregor: "Though he is at war with the civilisation where he was once a great figure, his enemies truly are not without but within the house of the soul. Because of that intimate conflict he is becoming a much greater writer. All his fiery arrows are sped from a bow bent in the passion of that intimate conflict. He makes his nobilities, as we all do, out of the struggle with what is base in us. I hope his battle will not be over too soon for him, for there is no one writes with such power. When he has expelled the demons in his soul he may become a saint. But, in that regained innocence of being, a great captain in the battle between darkness and light may be lost."

XIV

A GUSTY energy was in the air. Paul, stayed by rain at his door, looked up at the cyclopean world of cloud piled fabulously in precipices of lustrous pearl, cataracts of light, pools of blue fringed by glades of dazzling whiteness, miracles wrought by the wizard air, dissolving as swiftly as they were created, shedding from roots of cloud shadowy driftings of rain. A huge arch of seven quivering fires straddled across the valley. Beneath it, over wrinkled hollow and hill, waves of vivid green and gold rippled, chased incessantly by purple shadows. A hawk soared up as if it sought home in that cloudland. Brooding on the dissolving wonder Paul remembered Gregor's belief that all without us, whatever is seen on earth or in the heavens, even the noblest images, were but Maya. A despondency fell upon him. He went indoors. Here all about him was the work of seven years, since on that midsummer eve a new purpose had been given to his art. Were he and his friends like that hawk he had imagined, allured by a cloudland of images unsubstantial as those dissolving mists? A vast hope had been born among them, its father a dream, its mother a vision. It had been fed by intuition and imaginations. But might it not all be Maya? No embodiment of that hope had appeared in the world. He moved about among the paintings he had retained in the belief that, gathered together, in them finally might be seen the spirit of a new cycle. As he looked on them something of his despondency passed. Nature at least was living. The earth to him had been a mighty mother, majestically garrulous of the multitudes in her household, speaking to him in images which had come to him as he sat amid rocks on the mountain. Here were beings which were but coils of dazzling fire with faces of an ancient wisdom; dragon-crested divinities; beings like those spoken of in old mythologies; centaurs winged with flame, also the gentler beings who peered silently from the waters with blooms of delicate flame about their heads, or who rose, a glimmering brightness out of the rocks or emerged from the trees; sibyls breathing the mystical exhalations from earth while priests listened to the god-intoxicated utterance. Here, too, were images of a primaeval humanity which had drifted before him, and cities whose beauty was only in the eternal memory. Earth had spoken to him, not in words, but in that many-coloured speech of varied forms, and he had recorded it so far as his mastery over his art had enabled him. He moved from picture to picture, his despondency not altogether dispelled. The companionship between divinity and the human soul is unequal. While the divinity speaks to us we are exalted, but when the oracles are voiceless there is a sadness such as the unilluminated never know, for the spirit takes whom it wills, and it cannot be constrained even when to ourselves we are most solitary and need it most.

"I have been too much alone," he thought, and he understood why it was men and women sought each other, blotting out by one beloved face the majesty whose forms and faces are legion. Then he roused himself, and taking a canvas he began to work steadily on it. At last came a moment of relaxed attention and he had the sense he was no longer alone. There was a faint stir behind him. He turned. Leaning by the open door was a slender girl in a soft blue dress, her fair hair falling in clusters about the pure oval of her face. He rose, and as he moved to his visitor he saw a little silvery spark in the rich grey of the eyes, affectionate, doubtful, mocking, questioning. Then in an instant he remembered when he last saw that face.

"Olive! what ages since I saw you!"

They stood looking at each other with the questioning gaze of those who had been darlings of each other's hearts, and who wonder what years of separation have made of each other.

"I do not realise you as the little girl whose hair I used to ruffle."

"Are you not ashamed, you an artist, to remember that you did such a thing?" said that mocking affectionate voice. "It is as wicked, is it not—a sin against beauty—to disturb a tress as to burn the Alexandrine Library?" And at the saying of this he knew she had grown up and had run away from him and become another person, and he would have to know her all over again. There came to his mind the words of an Indian folk-song:

> She has become a woman, Her eyes have caught the dancing of her feet.

She came into the great room and walked about lightly from picture to picture.

"Oh!" she cried, almost becoming the

eager child again. She began to look at him with the old affection.

"You are just the same: you have painted the people who used to look out of the trees. But these I do not know." She pointed to some of the more majestic figures. "These are great people. You will tell me about them."

He began to speak hesitantly about what he was doing, for she did not know the long background of meditation out of which the images came. But she was intuitive and eager, and soon she had by a passionate inquisition extracted the wonder tale by which he and his friends were inspired.

"Oh, it is wonderful! And how, thinking all this, could you look so dejected as you were when I came in first. I watched you. You looked as if the universe had no light for you. Yet it is really lit up by a blaze of fairy torches."

"I think I have been too much alone lately. I have seen but little of my friends for some time. I have no ever-burning lamp within me, and my friends must feed the lamp with the oil of their ideas."

"You have been living too much among shadows and apparitions, Paul. No, not living.

It cannot be life when you are always looking at images, however noble. To have vision is not to live. I must bring Aoife here. If you see her all the world will turn to gold."

"The friend you called the Princess?"

"Yes. But she is more than a princess, more than a queen. She is like Helen of Troy, or one of the great heroines from the old epics. She sets fire to all about her."

"How have you come to love the thought of Helen and Troy burned?" he bantered her. "Is your ideal woman one who wrecks a civilisation?"

"It is we who make civilisations and we have the right to break them," the girl laughed. "Do you not realise that it is we who, with youth, with beauty, inspire all the hurried steps men take to the age of gold? I would like to overthrow the hateful civilisation we live in to-day. I could imagine Aoife leading against it armies she had made mad." She laughed at her own fantasy. "I see I must teach you world history as I see it. You only know what men have done. Civilisation began in some primaeval forest when a woman first plucked a flower and put it in her hair, and appeared like a spirit to her savage lover. Men would have been content with cave dwellings if women had not insisted on palaces, the counterpart in marble of a queen's beauty. The world will be reborn when some great beauty appears, a being so wonderful that men will feel life must be built anew around her. There should be a golden turbulence of rapture when a divine beauty passes by. But you are one of those people who are only fully awake when you are half asleep. That is, you go inside yourself and light candles there. But you must not go inward out of sight, Paul." She laid her hand on his arm and shook him with the lovely familiar petulance of her childhood.

Paul, delighted to have again the old intimacy, made himself humble with promises to be her slave as of old, but she would not have this.

"No, you must not. I love to twist people round my little finger. But if they go round I cannot endure them."

As he talked with the girl he felt some curiosity about that friend she called the Princess, for he divined she was talking a gallant language that was not learned in any school but had come from contact with some other who had brought her out of childhood into an incandescent girlhood.

"You are to come with me. Father and Mother have come back also. And I am never going away again. And you are to tell me everything about your wonderful boy. I am to become an initiate of the guild, am I not?"

XV

SOME little time after the return of Conaire's daughter, Felim broke in upon Paul one afternoon.

"Paul, you must stand up and gird yourself, for Conaire's prophecy is to be fulfilled. There are dragons and black enchantments to be overcome. I was with Gregor last evening, 'The great beast is aroused,' he said. 'The hunt will soon begin.' But it is the dragon who is to hunt us. There may now be only the lifting of an eyelid or the twitching of a tail, but the beast is gathering itself for a leap."

"What are you talking about?" asked Paul, lifting dream-cloudy eyes from his canvas.

"I say the lords of that monstrous mechanism, the State, have found the unrest in the world has its roots here. It is we, the spiritual anarchists, pagan poets and vagabond idealists, who have injected our own wildness into the social order. The slaves of the machine are becoming restless. No, it is not a passion for a new sharing out of wealth. The machine is efficient. Nobody is hungry now though the spirit may be starved. Everyone now is clothed in body though there may not be a rag of coloured fire about the psyche. No one is insecure, no one is homeless, unless they close their eyes to be bleak and homeless in the inner dark. It is the beginning of a spiritual renaissance. The State has nothing more to promise humanity, and when that is realised allegiance falls away. The spirit of man has lost itself in many illusions, and last of all it lost itself in the most pitiful illusion of any, the illusion of economic security and bodily comfort. These now fail to satisfy it, and there is nothing for it but spiritual adventures. Subconsciously it begins to remember ancient majesties, for in the midst of plenty without it is hollow and empty within."

"How are we the disturbers of the peace? I am glad to hear it. But I feel innocent for myself of any part in so good a work."

"Do you not know there are a score of fierce idealists in these regions spitting out their scorn on the comfortable world—Gregor the most powerful, whose books are read everywhere, and whose analysis cuts to the bone? Now there are warnings uttered about anarchists who would wreck the first perfectly organised society the world has known. The air quivers with anathemas from State and Church. They stir up passion which they can direct if need be. They can let loose on the idealists the wild beasts who kill in the name of the State. They can let loose a horde of wild fanatics who will rend us in the name of God."

"Your dragon is a very wild and glittering beast. But it does not terrify me. I wish you would speculate rather how those empty souls are to be made full. I ask about this, for before you came I was pondering over a man who left me an hour ago. I had thought of him as a magnificent unimaginative animal, but I think he suddenly conceived greatly about himself and I am responsible. I saw him first breaking stones lazily by the roadside. I never saw such a shapely creature. His body had the superb anatomies of the Adam of Michelangelo. Apollo in exile might have worn such a guise in dread of some more terrible divinity. As I imagined him so I painted him. He sat for me without showing the least interest in what I was making. Here is the picture. I call it 'A God in Exile.' "

The painting was of a man in rough patched trousers, a shirt open at breast and throat, while the sleeves were rolled up, showing those divine contours of throat, chest and arms of which Paul has spoken. The man was breaking stones, a humble task, but all about him, seen against the blue air, the fantasy of the artist had painted white, gold and rose-coloured flames swirling about the figure as if they blazed from a fire form only half hidden beneath the human disguise.

"What a magnificent creature!"

"When I had finished I drew him to see what I had made of him. He stood for a while looking silently, and then he drew himself up; said haughtily, 'What am I doing here!' and stalked out as if he was going to storm the heavens. Yet he might as conceivably in that new dilation of his being become the pursuer of nymphs as some of the ancient divinities were. When the gods cannot find the way back to their skies they too often descend in their thoughts to the fairer among the daughters of men."

"Ought I to be sorry for the nymph his eye singled out?" asked the poet. "He might be a wonderful lover. But I feel what you imply that our idealists have made the lives men live empty, but do not help those they have disillusioned to make a fulness."

"I find little imagination about life itself. I read books prophetic about the future. But the writers conceive only of more perfect mechanisms, not of a lordlier humanity. One will imagine airships of more electrical swiftness, or a force which might dissolve the bones of the world, or a boat which might sink under water to the harbours of sunken Atlantis. They imagine nothing about ourselves. Yet what could be more exciting than such speculations? Whether, for instance, in ten thousand years we may not all be able to send our thoughts as we will to distant friends and to have a like intimacy for ourselves: whether the psyche might not become so sensitive to the forces which pour on and through us that it might be able to reflect the multitudinous life of humanity in itself as the eye reflects a heaven of clouds and stars. Again, it is worth while brooding over whether we might not be able to extend consciousness into nature and interpret to ourselves the life on rock, water, earth or tree. It is conceivable also that there is an element of infinity at the root of every sense. It is manifest in the sense of sight which reaches out beyond sun and moon into the galaxies of stars and suns in the Milky Way. Might we not develop hearing to embrace the things beyond the seas and stars? Have not you and I heard voices of our friends speaking to us in intensity while they were yet many miles away? Have not you and I heard a musical vibration in the air and melodies from unseen players? It was not the physical ear heard but the power of hearing within. In the course of aeons that power might come to as wide a range as the power of sight and the myriad voices of nature be all intelligible to us. Our prophets do not speculate on human destiny, whether that other world which shines invisibly about us might not gradually become as native to us as this: whether we might not find the wings of the psyche unfolding and a spiritual body be born from the womb of this mortal body. We have in us in germ such powers as I spoke of. Their development is not incredible. Dilated to their perfection they would make all I have imagined possible for us."

"Yes, I know, you old wizard, when you talk about your pictures I can see them glowing in some aether about you. I look round but do not see an enchanter's wand. Yet you practise enchantments on myself and others."

The forms of imagination with Paul had

begun to glow as vividly as life. When talking about what he had seen he would sometimes conjure up the image and had been able to make it shine in the poet's mind. This was the casting of enchantments of which Felim had affectionately accused him. They were very close to each other these two, and thought was hardly born in one before it appeared in the mind of the other. Something of a like intimacy had grown up between these two and their other friends. Ideas flowed from mind to mind. Even without speech they became sharers of each other's wisdom. Paul and Felim began a speculation, whether this was the natural consequence of some identity of mood, or whether they were all bathed by some river of life whose ripples broke on the shores of the soul. Then the door was momentarily darkened and Conaire's daughter came in. She ran to Paul, taking his two hands and wringing them, her face pale and bright like a distraught angel, her lovely eyes agonised by some tragic happening.

"Oh, Paul, she has gone! Aoife has gone! I do not know where. She went away three days ago with some man, a stranger. She has not returned. She has sent no message. Oh, Paul, what can be done? What could have happened? You cannot feel it. You have never known her. To me she was like an angel of the Sun. I was only a little moon to her fire. Oh, if she should not come back! What can I do? What can we do?"

XVI

Very gently Paul spoke to the distressed girl: "Tell me how this happened."

"I had been with Aoife all day. She walked back with me the road over the hill. As we came near the top where the cromlech is, I thought I saw a light on the road, but there was no light. As we came to the cromlech I saw a tall figure of a man against the blue-green sky. He stood there until we were beside him. Then Aoife stopped. They looked at each other. He said to her:

"It is time for the play to begin. The chorus know their parts."

"I am ready," said Aoife.

"She turned then to me, kissed me and said 'Good-night, my child.' She seemed to me to have grown indescribably remote and great. I felt like a child who had been dismissed to its bed. I could say or do nothing. I watched them take the path down the valley, and oh, Paul, as they went there seemed a blue and golden light enveloping both, and they did not seem human to me but to be like some marvellous spirits journeying the earth. It is now three days since they went, and she has not returned. She has not even sent a message. What does it all mean? Who could the stranger be?"

"How did he appear to you?"

"I thought at first he was a peasant. He was dressed like one very simply. His head was bare and a great mane of yellow golden hair rose up from his forehead and fell to his shoulders. It was like a lion's mane. His face I thought very noble, and his eyes, when he turned them on me for an instant, had a light in them which seemed to come from something further and deeper than the sky. As he turned away with Aoife I saw what seemed like a violin-case slung over his shoulders."

"It is the child of your vision, the boy on the mountain. Mary's Fairy Fiddler now grown up," said Felim, who had listened intently. "Dream and vision are to be justified. The play is to begin. It must be a great play to be heralded by miracles in so many souls. We are the chorus, we and others we do not know, who have been prepared for many years to play our parts. Do not be distressed," he said to the girl. "They are immortals. They do not err and lose their way in life as we do. You should be exalted rather, being a character in so great a tale, a tale which may be told for ages about these two. What did you want your princess to become? To settle down as the beloved of someone of her own rank, to bear him children, have a brief summer of beauty and be forgotten. For what she does now I think she will never be forgotten. These twain may be a pivot round which the imagination of the world will wheel to new spiritual destinies."

"Yes," said the girl. "I feel she must take her own way. There is something great, unheard of before, in Aoife. She might have been a queen, but she laughed at an infatuated young prince who thought his rank made him an equal. If she reverses the tale of Cophetua's queen I will not be saddened. She would know it was a King of men in disguise. I only become wild knowing nothing."

"She does not stoop choosing such a companion, who is, I am sure, great beyond our dreaming of him. Already there are many whose imaginations, they know not why, follow him as planets circle around the sun. Do not be deceived by the guise in which he appears. 'The wise ones assume excellent forms in secret.' Did an Avatar ever sit on a throne? Have they not always gone about the world as vagrants? How could they make us believe in the riches of their world if they did not despise the riches of this?"

"You truly believe, then," she asked of Paul, "that this is the strange boy of whom you spoke to me?"

"I am certain as Felim of this."

"Oh, I am already lighter of heart. I feel it must be so and this is that unimagined thing I always felt must be her destiny. I have no heart sadness now, only an excitement of spirit. But I am too excited to talk. I must be alone with all you have said. You remember, Paul, the stone on which I used to sit when I was a little girl and tried to puzzle things out for myself, and I would not have even you with me until everything was clear. I am going there again. I am sure the hills will not let me think falsely. They will not tell me a lie."

She went from them. Perhaps because they, like her, had gone on some inner quest, they did not speak to each other about what she had told them. Felim, watching the girl flitting through the wood, began to speak of her.

"She has a spirit flashing like quicksilver. I am glad you initiated her into our mystery, for she herself must be one of the chorus. I remember her a small girl. You were away then. She had come back from her school on holiday. She brought me into the wood where you painted those dancing figures, and made me tell her every secret of the universe that I knew. To please her was a poet's whole-time work without holiday. I had begun to think of other things. She saw my lapse and stamped at me indignantly like a young queen. I was delighted with that imperiousness which brought me to her feet. It was about her I wrote those verses I call 'Distraction.' Do you remember?

"I lapse from her sweet play. Although
My heart had hardly beat
For a dream instant, the wild child
Stamps with imperious feet.

"Wind-quickened shook the forest boughs,
Green glitterings died and came.
O'er her young stormy beauty broke
Ripples of shade and flame.

"I wake, my lovely child, I wake.
I fly thy slave to be,
Forgive, O voices from the deep,
Yet come again to me.

"I think she has the genius for living and she may find her way into the heart of our mystery more than any of us. We turn what we imagine into poetry and art. She will live what she imagines. You and I would not dare to follow those two on their wanderings. But that girl will not rest until she has found them. She will be like a shadow following their footsteps until her heart, not her head, finds what it sought for."

XVII

THE spiritual are swift transmitters of thought. Among those mystical communities, which had sought refuge from a civilisation they hated amid the mountainy regions, rumours of a spiritual excitement created by two divinely beautiful visitors began to spread, as in India knowledge of distant happenings spreads from city to city. The rumours began weeks after the vanishing of Aoife. They came first from the far south. To those who heard the rumours it seemed as if, after dark aeons that had lain like frost on the heart, the ice was melting and the spring of a new golden age was stealing upon the earth. The strangers had come to those communities who were creating through the arts a culture in harmony with their spiritual intuitions. By the presence of these two the days had been coloured with a rich wonder. Something, rumour at first did not say what, had been added to drama, dance and song. Then came stories of men and women raised above themselves in some transfiguration so that they saw each other in some shining way in moonlit dances in forest glades, in dances which had been taught them by the mystic visitors, for as they swayed in the dance their feet came to be lighter, to have the gay movement of dream. As the dancers looked at each other, they saw bodies no longer lit by the moonlight but which seemed to glow from within and to be radiant with starry colours and plumes of delicate flame. In their enchantment they were god and goddess to each other. It seemed natural in that moment of exaltation. Surprise came only when the music died out and dance and dream had ended, and the strangers had gone away from them, leaving the dancers to sorrow and wonder over the dying glory in themselves. From another came a tale of a music played amid the rocks which melted those who heard it in its ecstasy, so that their own being became a music, and nature itself a divine tone in which earth and heaven were dissolved. Others told of lovely genii seen in the air who seemed to wait on the two strangers, and who made a shining drama of their words so that the meanings were exalted. And as the days passed, Paul, Felim and Olive could follow the route of the mystic revellers which brought them nearer and nearer to those who waited their coming in a passion of longing. Through those days Conaire's daughter had been still. The distress she felt at first at the vanishing of her friend had gone. It may be she was moved by the belief of her friends that we have only to be ourselves and what is our own must come to us and we cannot lose what is our own. But one morning that restraint was gone. A fairy excitement invaded her. She took the road over the mountains southward. Her body seemed to herself light as air. She felt as one might who knows her feet are god-guided, and though she did not know what would be her way, she went happily on her blind and rapt wandering.

On the evening after she came into the room where Paul was with Felim and said:

"I have seen them."

They remained silent but turned intent eyes on her. They knew without asking who those were she spoke of, and waited for her speech.

"When I woke yesterday morning I felt like a boat whose anchor had been lifted and the wind was blowing it out of harbour. Yet I did not know where to go or what I was to do. I waited for some understanding and then I felt as if Aoife had taken me by the hand. I walked away over the mountain road. I knew I was called to her, that I was going to meet her. I was not tired by the long road, nor was I uncertain, and that fairy exaltation never left me until at evening I saw about twenty-five or thirty people in a glade and above the glade the hill rose steeply. Aoife was there. I sat down beside her. She patted my hand but said nothing. They were all listening to a half-musical play composed by a young man I heard spoken of as Rory. He and his sister were both actors in the play. I thought it beautiful. In it the soul was led by music to the fairy world. There were songs by invisible singers hidden behind rocks or trees on the hills. Song and music became more ethereal as they came from the heights. But the real wonder came when the voices had died upon the hills, for there then sounded a melody played on a violin, a music not born out of any human emotion, but the melody of aether itself, a tapestry of sound wavering between earth and heaven. I felt if that magical curtain lifted I would be in Paradise. When it died inaudible by the ear it was still audible by the spirit. I saw the boy and girl as in a trance holding each other's hands while they listened to a finale more marvellous than anything they had imagined. When that music ended, the man you spoke of as Aodh came down the slope to Aoife. Some went away at once as if they could not endure human speech after so much beauty and must be alone to caress the memory. But Aodh and Aoife moved on together; and, as in trance where one is moved from beyond oneself, I followed with six or seven others. The young musician and his sister, Mark and Mary were among them. But for what seemed like a spell laid upon us I think we would have been too awed to follow. We came to a mossy hollow on the hillside just above the road. It overlooked a valley which was growing vast and vague and blue in the twilight. We sat down on moss or stones. I felt as we do in dreams where consciousness stirs and we know our waking selves are in the dream world and we see wonders unrolled before us in the wizardry of dream. I was in some way beyond dream. I heard Aoife speaking about the young man's musical fantasy, and how it was right to make beautiful images because we became what we imagine. The realists who think they are closer to truth are no less depicting a world created by imagination though it is begotten by dark desires. The universe itself was nothing but Imagination ceaselessly creative. The Imagination and Will which uphold it are in us also, so that we can make our own world and transfigure it out of the glory still within us. We were not what we seemed but children of the heavens. The body even is a palace all marvellous within. It has secret radiant gateways opening inward to light. It has wings which could be unfolded. All the precious fires of Elohim are co-mingled in us. She said there were many who came in the past from that heaven world of light, divine poets, who made known the paths between earth and heaven. This they did less by speech than by opening the blind eyes, and showing images of gods and immortals in a clear, immovable and blessed light. As I listened, my eyes, which had been fixed on Aoife, passed for a moment to the blue twilight air which was over the valley. It seemed to me there was a secret shining in it like that blessed light she spoke of, and I saw in it radiant forms in harmony with her words. When she spoke of the body as lit with precious fires, a figure upon that mystic screen, which had been shadowy, began to glow, and it became transparent, a dazzling opalescence, and there were lights in it like sunfire for brilliancy. It was so glorious that I remembered the prophet who said of the soul that it had been on the holy mountain of God and walked amid the stones of fire where every precious stone was its covering. Then that radiant psyche itself became transfigured and was changed to a dark divine majesty, and as I looked I heard her speaking of the return of the Son to the Father. She told tales of those divine poets, Apollo, Krishna, Lugh, and as she spoke there were majestic images in that shining aether as if they were all still living in the eternal memory. I cannot now speak of all I saw there. I must brood over it lest it fades from me like a dream when we wake. But there were figures on that aether like some you, Paul, had painted, and I knew that you had looked into that shining glass. Through it all Aodh sat silently, but I thought he was the magician who made these living pictures to glow in the twilight air. When Aoife ended she and Aodh went away from us. I went home with Mary and stayed with her that night. What I tell you is but a little part of mysteries which are too great for my understanding. I feel very young, a child who has strayed into the company of immortals and heard them talking in their own speech and it was too high for me."

She looked at them silently for a moment and then left them, going to Conaire's house.

XVIII

"THAT young girl has been burdened with great mysteries," said the poet. "You were right to question nothing, to ask no more. These are things which are lost through speaking of them. It would be wrong to break her mood of wonder. In solitude, in that mood, she may recall and make those marvels all her own. When she has made them secure in memory she will tell us about them and I am sure she will understand. I do not believe vision is vouchsafed to any without its interpretation. I think she told us what she did lest it might fade away or some cloud come between her waking mind and the light which was born in her. I think that you and I understand that imparting of mystical vision. Before Aodh and Aoife went on their wanderings, images like those Olive spoke of shone before you in reverie. I am less of a seer than you are. Yet I have long had the feeling that there was some shepherd of my spiritual life. It is difficult to give reasons for this conviction. Nor do you want them. You have the same certitude. But you are an artist and can give permanence to your vision, and those who have vision can say 'Yes, I have seen just such forms.' But moods are bodiless things, and however we speak of them we cannot compare them with the moods of others, so that we may be made certain of the identity of moods and that they come from the same source. A few days ago that Spirit which made its promise to man, 'I will not leave thee or forsake thee,' renewed to me that ancient promise, and I seemed in my solitude to be with that which endures from everlasting to everlasting. What can we bring back from these visitations? We are dark and blind with a glory of being. But the words that fly up to the brain in our intoxication are too feeble a net to catch Leviathan. What have we to give to others? Only a few half-mad words! What had I to give to others but this with no precise revelation in it, nothing to make a philosophy out of.

"The pool glowed to a magic cauldron
O'er which I bent alone.
The sun burnt fiercely on the waters;
The setting sun;
A madness of fire. Around it
A dark glory of stone.

"O mystic fire!
Stillness of earth and air!
That burning silence I
For an instant share.
In the crystal of quiet I gaze
And the god is there.

"Within that loneliness
What multitude!
In the silence what ancient promise
Again renewed!
Then the wonder goes from the stones,
The lake and the shadowy wood.

"The mood in that is any man's heritage. A lonely herdsman in Tartary, a hunter on Peruvian hills, might meet the All-pervading. It is not by brooding on such illuminations we will discover the guidance of the spiritual Shepherd we imagine."

"Why not?" asked Paul.

"I think we must look for it in a quality of thought, a character or tendency in many people such as historians find in their summing up of past cultures, who know that beauty was the mask the ancient Greeks sought to lift to discover deity, who find a common mind in the Egyptians, the Hindus, the Chaldeans or the Chinese. If there is a new outbreathing from the Earth Spirit, as we imagine, it may be we are too intimate with it for understanding. It is the spiritual air we breathe and it cannot now be objective to us. A little longer waiting and what is hidden may rush out and act through many men and speak through many voices. I talk quietly with you, but all the while the psyche in me is dancing the gayest dance. I am as blind and mad and happy as I was when I was a boy and rolled naked in the wet grasses or drew the living air into myself or hugged the earth, having found they were all living. No child ever laid its head against its mother's breast with more tender an intimacy. To-day I feel just as blind and mad and happy. Our dream is coming true. All the things which seemed remote and fabulous, tales of a golden age, of gods mingling with men, things sunken from belief on remote horizons of time, now seem to rise to us, to be true once more. I shall never be able to transfigure myself into a grandeur to meet them as people do when kings and princes come to their city. I could only be like that acrobat who did all his tricks in tumbling before the shrine of the Virgin as his best worshipping of the goddess. I have, alas, no skill as an acrobat. Come with me, Paul, and we will be forerunners. I will chant my poems and you will carry your pictures of the gods and I will cry 'These come after us!

These come after us! Look out for the immortals.'"

"It is easy for you who carry your songs in your head. I could not carry my pictures. I must be a pavement artist. Give me a smooth pavement and I will colour it with fairy."

That inward awe and excitement of spirit they felt translated itself into a light-hearted fantasy of thought and speech. How should they greet the divine strangers if they met them on the highway knowing that these were immortals in human guise? Should they prostrate themselves before the divinities?

"No! no!" said Felim. "We would do none of these things. What are the gods but elder brothers to us. We are of the same lineage. I will pay reverence to those who transcend me, but I will not abase myself. I do not think the immortals wish any of their kin, however lowly, to degrade themselves into being flatterers of their majesty as the church-goers do, hoping to propitiate a vain deity. How could the gods delight in seeing us abase ourselves before them as worms or miserable sinners? We should be natural with the immortals as the children in a great house are natural with their elders. Anyhow we will think more truly when, like Olive, we each enter our own solitude. I leave you to yours," and went away.

But Paul was not to be left long to his solitude, for Michael Gregor came to him and began to speak to him about a plot he had discovered to tie together the loose ends of society, bringing all the refugees and vagrants from civilisation under the mechanism of the State.

"Our freedom is dangerous to it."

XIX

"I DECLARE to Heaven, which does not mind in the least, that there must be a devil in one if one is to understand the diabolism of the State. The State is the devil, or rather a multitude of devils. Its name is legion. It has been questing all about this region to find the fountain of unrest in society. At first men went about alone. But yesterday I found some dark and surly brutes together, exotic to this country, and I guess by that old devil not yet dead in me, that they intend some devilry. There is a festival in the village to-night. I am guessing they will be there and for some bad purpose. I am going to watch them."

He walked restlessly about the room, casting a glance every now and then at the paintings.

"I am not an initiate of your guild, though you, Felim, Conaire and our other friends are more to me than any others. I have still something of that ancient devil in me which makes me an alien. But you fit in somewhere with all I hold in spirit to be true and good. Even these majestical images which you have painted and which my reason declares to be self-begotten fantasies, born out of a poetical nature—like that, and like nothing else in heaven or earth—now when I look at them, somehow beyond reason, catch at my spirit and seem in some unplumbed deep of me to symbolise a reality. I say to myself, after all, why should not the universe, through all its infinitudes, hold such beings even if my outer mind can't find a glimmer of substance in the imaginations? I am lately feeling more of a difference between inner and outer. I am with you against the world. I would fight for you in the hope that your dreams might after all be true. I might after death wake amid heavenly things and be hailed there as a martyr who had died for a beauty he had never seen. You who are naturally spiritual can adventure into fantasy. I, most of whose life was spent chasing illusions, can find peace only in imagining a deep of being beyond sight or sound. My heart holds to something that may be cold to you, too vast or too vague to warm the heart. I am not a poet like Felim, who can put into words the secret things in his soul. But I found in a poem of his a mood which comes close to that which is my comfort:

"The skies were dim and vast and deep
Above the vale of rest.
They seemed to rock the stars to sleep
Beyond the mountain's crest.

"I sought for graves I had mourned, but found
The roads were blind. The grave,
Even of love, heart-lost, was drowned
Under time's brimming wave.

"Huddled beneath the wheeling sky
Strange was my comfort there :
That stars and stones and love and I
Drew to one sepulchre."

"The mood in that is a current that sets to the great deep. You are as near to it as any of us," said Paul.

"I have lately allowed myself to dream a little. I found the old devil in me was not so clever as he was, and did not seize upon the beauty to hide himself in it. I feel a little high and beyond myself to-night. Maybe it is because I can drink the cup of dream and find no poison in the cup, not a heartache in it. What is it in me? Is it a long winter changing to spring? I am elated as I have not been since I was an innocent boy. Or is it the magic of earth? But I must go. I have to track my devils."

"I will come with you," said Paul. He was unusually stirred about his friend, and wondered what had brought about the change, the exaltation of mind he felt about Gregor. For a while there was silence, except for the sound of their feet on the hard road.

"The men of science tell us that almost the instant a football sounds here the vibration ripples about the Pleiades. Would it be right if we interpreted their esoteric mathematic to mean that our least motions send a quiver through omnipresence? I mistrust any speculation which cannot be stated in the natural speech of man. When thought hides itself in monstrous equations, or in pedantic dialectic, I am sure it is misshapen thought. I am sure it must be useless for man. Yet, if what we do runs through infinitude, we in turn must be penetrated by terrors and grandeurs pouring on us and through us out of the vastness. All wisdom must be uttered to us. You and I carry the universe in our packs. But blind and deaf to it all, I am hunting some low brutes who I suspect are sent here on some devilish mission."

"You may be wiser than you know. That intuition of yours about devils in your neighbourhood may be the one thing out of all your subconscious omniscience that you most need to know."

A man and girl hurrying, passed them on

the way. Paul heard the girl's voice in a strange eagerness saying to the man, "I hear the two will be there," and on the hearing of this a sudden excitement fell upon him also.

"We will follow these," he said. "I think they must be going to that festival you spoke of."

Paul was wondering whether those long sequences of vision, dream and intuition were coming to a consummation. To his dilated consciousness the night seemed dense with majestic beings intent on all that was happening. The road turned and widened and he saw a crowd, a dark blur of forms thrown into a silhouette by a lantern held low by someone beyond. He heard the sound of a voice which thrilled him while he was yet too remote to hear its meanings. He hurried to be closer, and above that dark blurring of heads he saw, illuminated by the low-swung light, two faces which remained with him for ever. They overtopped the crowd. There was a godlike head, a mane of golden hair rising above the brow and falling to the shoulder. What ancientness there was in its youth! And beside it the face of a woman. Paul thought of all the goddesses men had imagined in stone or colour for its peer and could not find it. He saw with the greatest lucidity the contours of face, the light of the eyes. It was only afterwards he knew that he could not have seen what he remembered with such distinctness by that flickering lantern light, and there must have been spirit perception added to bodily vision. Aoife was speaking and he began to hear what was said, something about a return to ever-living nature, how men would leave their dark cities, their dead religions, their grey churches and twilight sanctuaries, turning to the altars of the hills, soon to be lit up as of old. "Ah, my darlings, you must fight and you must suffer. You must endure loneliness, the coldness of friends, the alienation of love, warmed only by the interior hope of a future you must toil for but may never see, laying down in dark places the foundations of that holy earth of prophecy, with the face of the everlasting beauty glowing through all its ways, divine with terrestrial mingling till God and the world be one." Then someone gave a signal. There was a rush of dark figures towards Aodh and Aoife, and to Paul's imagination an unearthly blackness seemed to envelop those hurrying figures and made them seem ministers of some divinity of evil.

"Oh, the devils," he heard Gregor speaking, as he rushed forward. Paul followed. He saw the head of Aodh with its glittering golden mane rise more lionlike. A light seemed to ray from him. Then Paul was thrust on one side. A surly voice growled, "Keep out of this. Don't interfere." Unheeding he hurried after Gregor. A bludgeon fell on him and he knew no more of what happened until he came at last to an agonising consciousness. He was in his own room. There was a fierce aching in his head. He saw Conaire's daughter beside him. Her eyes were on him. They held so much anguish that he thought of angels in torture. When she saw his eyes open she knelt down by the couch on which he lay and took both hands.

"Oh, Paul, you at least are living." Then he heard that Gregor was dead, the first martyr for a faith he did not hold. Aodh and Aoife had vanished. His mind was still so cloudy and confused that he could hardly follow her tale of what happened. The lantern was extinguished. There was a rush of those dark brutal strangers, and then a flight after the deed was done. When the crowd, so rudely broken up, drew itself together there was no trace at all of that lordly twain about whom had gathered so much wonder and mystery. There was a long search, but, living or dead, they had vanished. The girl, faltering in her tale, broke down: "Oh, Paul, what has become of Aoife?" She wept kneeling beside him, and he, shaken and dazed and not yet understanding fully, could only stretch out a trembling hand to caress feebly the lovely, bowed and weeping head.

XX

A YEAR had passed since Aodh and Aoife had gone from earthly knowledge of them. Conaire, his daughter and Carew were with Paul. They sat close to the open door of the great room crowded with his paintings. Through waving branches the descending sun shot flickering fingers of fire through the door, which touched those who sat there and the mystic figures on the walls so that they glowed momentarily with an almost superphysical light.

"It is little more than a year," said Conaire, "since that which began in our world as a dream and a vision fulfilled itself and departed. Already the story is becoming one of the great legends of the world like the story of Radha and Krishna or the tale of Helen. It is a fairy tale made real, a reversal of the tale of Cophetua. A beautiful woman who might, if she wished, have been a queen, and a peasant mystic, a child of earth, began a companionship. For a few months they came into the lives of others and created a spiritual wonder as they passed. Already pilgrims from many countries walk these mountainy roads, following what has been called the Route of the Mystic Revellers, and if they meet any who had seen Aodh or Aoife they look on such people with awe as people who with bodily eyes had looked upon immortals. Now a great temple is to be built at the place where the two disappeared, and in this are to be placed whatever in the arts, music, poetry or philosophy seems to have been born out of that spiritual wonder, or out of prescience of the coming of Aodh and Aoife, the paintings of Paul, the sculpture of Mark and his pupils. Every story of Aodh and Aoife, whatever was known of them is being reverently collected. A very rich culture has been born about us, a culture in which we find our own inmost intuitions reflected, a culture so harmonious in its parts that it seems almost the product of one mind. These strangers also who come here from whatever distant continents seem to me intimates of the soul, as much so as if they had lived with us for years and had sat by the hearth with us and shared our dreams. A moment after our meeting we can talk to them in that secret language of the heart we use with those who have been comrades in the spirit a long time together. It would almost appear that the needles of spiritual being pointed to this region and the travellers were guided to it."

"It is not only these later pilgrims who were so guided," said Felim. "Were not we ourselves brought together by spiritual gravitation? You were born here. But what was it brought Paul or Mark or Gregor, or indeed most of these who are our spiritual kinsmen? I know I myself came on what seemed the whim of an instant, and I found in a few days more who could understand my language than I had known before in my lifetime. How did it happen? Were we called inwardly? Or is there some law in the being in which we live and move which draws affinities together, just as in ourselves if any mention Paris or Rome or San Francisco, all that we have known of these cities, all our memories of them, awake silently, come together and swim up in consciousness. Was the incarnation of a divine being so powerful a magnet that it drew secretly to itself those who had begotten in themselves a fire akin to that great fire. Or did the avatar choose its own, having an inward vision of the colours with which the soul shines so that he knew in whom there was a spark which could be blown into flame? How did Jesus or Buddha choose those who became disciples? John knew the prophet of the spirit because he was himself a seer, and he saw an aureole like wings around the head of the Avatar and knew what golden lamps were lit behind the brows. I can imagine a wider vision which could discern multitudes, and know to what order of being they belong by the light or the darkness about them. I am not going to rebel against being called. But I would like to believe that in some deep of my being I saw the Avatar and came to him by my own will. I dislike the idea of being only the slave of light."

"I have never understood what is meant by those who talk of natural or spiritual law," said Conaire. "For whatever takes place seems to me to be but movement within divine being, and what people speak of as laws are but intuitions about the mode of that being. There is something in me which leads me to speculate beyond the doctrine of affinities, which yet is true; or beyond your idea that certain people are called, as I think they are, for I share in your intuition against all being ordered and that we are but the slaves of light. I think that at the root of our being we will what we do; that we choose our lives as in that myth in the Republic Plato imagines Ulysses choosing a quietness into which he would be reborn. Prometheus, as many suppose, is not one being, but symbolises a host of beings who are ourselves, and that we, like the Titan, come to earth with a fire born in the heavens, and that like him we foresaw all that would happen. The Gnostics said of Christ that He was in all humanity, and the myth of His taking on Himself the burden of the sins of the world would, if this interpretation is true, have the same meaning as the Promethean myth. There are many such intimations by the seers and prophets that what we endure was brought about by our primal will and was foreseen. I have always been in revolt against any imagination of life which makes us the puppets of law or destiny or of beings outside ourselves. It was out of a like mood was born the indignation which made the Persian poet cry out:

> "What! from his helpless creatures be repaid
> Pure gold for what he lent us dross allayed!
> Sue for a debt we never did contract
> And cannot answer. O the sorry trade!

Whether the law seems benign to us or the divinity favourable to our desires, to have no part in our destiny is unpleasing to me. I feel that in some secrecy of our being we are the choosers, that we willed what we have done. Even if the outer being finds itself outcast, in prison, hopeless or suffering, the inner spirit knew what wisdom or power it would have through undergoing just such things. The moment of willing our fate may be at the first outbreathing of the universe. Or, before we are reborn, we may, as Plato suggests, choose the circumstance of our lives. Or it may be, as the Indian seers hold, we go back every night, when we are beyond dream, to a state of spirit-waking, where for an instant we are truly ourselves and have communion with the gods. There again we may will what is to be done, though when we waken we may not remember at all what majesties we have known; and from this state the soul receives impulses which are surprising to itself but which it yet obeys. My intuition is with the Indian seers and I think we have always freedom of choice. If this philosophy is true, we are co-workers with divinities, what we endure we have willed; and if we find ourselves miserable or helpless here, we are not condemned to that pain by a deity outside ourselves. It is rather like the agony one suffers who has gone heroically into a fiery pit to rescue others, and there is a spiritual gain from it."

"That is a noble and consoling doctrine," said Paul. "It implies in regard to the Avatar that we had enlisted under the banner of one who was greater than ourselves. If we were called, it was because we had already chosen. But what was it was devised? Is there any wisdom of past seers about the labours of Avatars. Were those who so excited our imagination to be called by that name? If so, what was their peculiar message. All those who spoke out of the divine world revealed some wisdom never before apprehended. What spiritual inheritance is made ours by the coming of Aodh and Aoife?"

XXI

"In India the seers spoke of the Manus, who were the spiritual guides of humanity, as thinking out in their high regions the religions of the future. I am not a seer, but I had long ago, as you may remember, a dream which in its fantasy embodied the same idea. If we can imagine such beings having a vision of life from within, brooding over a race, or over humanity, then those moods which were most widely diffused among people might be the moods whose exaltation or transfiguration into heavenly counterparts it would be the art of Avatar to bring about. How are we to discover such a mood in ourselves? Fletcher makes the most heroic character in his play say of Deity:

> His hidden meaning dwells in our endeavours.

It is by intimate confession among ourselves how the universe has been changed to us, what secret lovely desires we have in our hearts, that we may discover a common intent, and come to believe that impulses springing up deeply within us were messages from gods. It may be that we shall never know what will be plain to those who come after us. Every wave of time has its own glitter. How few really enter intimately into the consciousness of those who come after them. I am the elder here, and even my dearest"—Conaire looked affectionately at his daughter—"has a thousand moods which I can only adore without understanding. She has been baptized with radiant fires while I have only known the lustration of water. She acts by impulses from within while I only philosophise. I am all eagerness to leap from my wave of time here. But even if I could be as young as the youngest, I am certain that the Avatars plan not for their own day here, but for long centuries. What in them is a divine intensity or fulness may be unrolled in time into an infinity of moods and ideas evolving new beauties like a flower in its growth, and this through many generations. In Plato perhaps came a full flowering of the conception of beauty in its very essence as Deity, and the seed of that idea may have been cast into his race a thousand years before. We surmise behind many statements a long ancestry of speculation. In one of the Vedic hymns the poet speculates whether the most high seer that lives in highest heaven can be self-conscious: 'Perhaps he knows, perhaps even he knows not.' Was that born as a sudden intuition or did the doubt arise out of long and subtle speculations upon the nature of Deity. It is possible too that what is a long history for us may, to a being rooted in a timeless world, be but an instant in which he acts consciously, not in that moment only but through ages which are hereafter to us but now to him, and the meanings of all be known only in the history of a culture which has come to its culmination."

While Conaire was speaking three people had entered the room silently and had seated themselves, Mark, Cluborn, one of the pilgrims from the New World who with the romantic generosity of his race had made possible the building of that temple of which the philosopher had spoken, a man who had made himself loved by a shining simplicity and friendliness. The third was the boy Rory Lavelle, whose uncle, also a poet, had perished in a revolt against the world state many years before.

"Is this a symposium on Aodh and Aoife?" asked Mark. "May we listen?"

"Yes, and take part if you will. I was going to say that around every Avatar in the past a civilisation had arisen, and in that civilisation was the reflection of his spirit, and how difficult it was to discover by brooding over a few years meanings which were unrolled through long centuries. I am doubtful myself whether the creation of a civilisation was in the will of Aodh or Aoife."

"Why," asked Felim impetuously, "must we assume that to create a civilisation was in the plan? Why inspire those who hate civilisation and have fled from it? Might not the purpose be rather to bring us into communion with a living nature. What has civilisation brought us but the triumph of the great heresy of separateness between ourselves and nature? Has there been any civilisation which did not defend itself within walls of clay or stone from the Earth Spirit as from an enemy? I see your reproachful eyes," he said to Conaire. "I have wronged you. Brick, stone, mortar, cement or steel are not necessary ingredients in your civilisation. If three people are together under the skies and the soul is conscious between them, that is civilisation." The old man smiled. "Let us think what has been born among us here. Is it not that nature has become living to our imaginations, is itself an imagination of the lordliest kind which envelops us and cherishes us who turn to it as to an elder brother? Has not earth been tender towards us? Are not sunlight, twilight, colour, form, element, melted into meanings so that they seem but voices out of that ever-living nature? Does not the very air we breathe seem at times to be the Holy Breath? Are we not for ever passing into what we contemplate? Have not solid earth, stone and hill become transparent at times to us? As we become purified we have vision of a hitherto unknown virgin beauty and are awed and hallowed by the vision. Are we not made happy and blessed by a love breathed through the dark clay? There grows up a magic between men and women when they love. Has not such a magic grown between us and nature, and the heart chokes with love as it does when it is nigh the fulfilment of desire? Do we not go out at times from ourselves, our being expanded, so that we seem to mix with the life in nature as if we permeated it and had come together in the infinite yearning of centre and circumference for each other? In that co-mingling of natures the gates of the heart are unbarred for there is nought to defend. Our darkness becomes brimming with stars. Everything becomes holy. Even the dust becomes precious as light." He turned to Paul. "Is not this what your seership revealed? A nature living from depths to heights. What was it happened to you and to us after that secret baptism of the spirit was received? Is it not because of that baptism you cannot paint a valley but it seems as living as the quickness behind the brows? It is this sense of the universe as spiritual being which has become common between us, that a vast tenderness enfolds us, is about us and within us. It was that intimacy the Avatar came to quicken, he who had no roof over his head but the sky, to whom earth itself was hearth and home; and who knows what blazing pavements these rocky roads may not have been to his vision! There was that intimacy between man and nature at the beginning of the world. In the Golden Age we were not separate but one. Then we were half divine. What has been happening to us is that we have been lapsing back into that intimacy. Unawares almost we have strayed into the heavenly household and feel we are of divine kin. Outside that we are but men and women, and oh, how unhappy and how little are our joys."

"Yes, we have all come to that faith," said Paul, "though the ecstasy does not leap upon us all so swiftly in contemplation. But I would say that this vision of an exhaustless ever-living nature is in all the ancient religions, is indeed what makes any religion possible, and what we were seeking for has a particular character or message. When Socrates has the vision of Deity as Beauty in its very essence; when the exalted seers of the Upanishads cry out, 'This is the real, this is the true'; or when another seer cries out that God is love, they utter words which guide the soul for generations after them. Yet they were all speaking about that same profundity of being as Felim. What we are looking for is not a new heaven but a new ladder by which we may climb from earth to the ancient skies."

XXII

"A NEW upward-leading path! But how shall we find that when so little has been told, though so much has been imagined. We have to ask ourselves what do we know certainly about Aodh. That he creates by imagination what he desires. Even as a child he said of those about him, 'I imagine them wearing gay colours and they begin to wear them. I imagine them dancing in curves like the water and they begin to dance.' What attribute do we give to gods? That they are creative. In what way? Krishna says of himself, 'I am born through my own maya, the mystic power of self-ideation.' If Aodh be a divinity come to earth, he lived here as he lived in the heavens, creating what he desired. There he may have been one of the high rulers of the spheres. Here instinctively as a child he began to use the same power, but as a child might use it. Soon he would be finding his way inward to light. He would reawaken to his own divinity. He would use greater powers. What was he doing while Aoife told those tales of gods and avatars? Was he not creating images of them on the spiritual air? Do any of us know all he did? If he had that greatness we imagine of him, we could hardly with our highest consciousness touch more than the lower fringes of a being towering into infinity. Certainly he was quickening imagination in us. Once I was walking along the sands at night, and I suddenly felt as if I was pelted with fire. I was so beaten by the fiery storm that I was nigh to fainting because of its almost unendurable intensity. For years afterwards that seed of fire cast into my soul was blossoming into imaginations, indeed into all I have done. Every imagination in itself was a spur to further imagination. It was, I believe, to kindle a creative imagination that Aodh was born into our sphere. What has happened to life? It has been frozen in monstrous mechanisms. The creative genius which is the soul of man, his very self, has become atrophied. What has united us all here? Were we not all rebel against those mechanisms? What is it but a delight in the creative arts links us with those who are our spiritual kinsmen? What is important in this is the mood of creation itself rather than what is created. It is in the ecstasy of creation that we are made aware of divine deeps in our own being. When that ever-living nature glowed before Felim, was it the vision which gave life? Did it not rather give impulse to creation, to transmute bodiless spirit into beauty, into melody? You felt master of your power when the wild beautiful words flew upward to be molten together into images, emotion and thought. You were writing poetry while Mark was modelling his imaginations. Was there not some magical change taking place inwardly, something more wonderful than the poem or the statue? It was the soul becoming itself in creation, using its god-descended power. We have in potency all the powers of the ancestral self. It is by their use we re-enter the heavens. What is the universe but ceaseless creation by the congregation of divine powers. We have through long ages imagined ourselves into what we are. We have now to imagine ourselves back into light. The most mystic of all Scriptures says: 'On that path to whatever place one would travel, that place one's own self becomes.'"

"Do we imagine ourselves what we wish to be?"

"Yes. Here in this world where time beats slowly, it is long ere we so change ourselves. But in that mid-world as we know from dream the creative power acts in an instant. We are not yet masters of the dream consciousness. When we create there we project in an instant images, scenes and incidents. But we have not yet learned consciously to use the power of imagination in that world upon ourselves, equalling ourselves to the gods. What did Aodh do to those he moved among? I think he brought a wisdom of imagination, a wisdom changing as we rise from one plane of being to another. Here it may begin with the imagination acting outward, creating music, picture, architecture, sculpture, poetry. It may be seen in the beauty of arts and crafts. As we ascend within ourselves, the imagination begins to act inwards, and as it acts our being becomes incandescent."

"How would that inward imagination act?"

"How, but as Thrice Great Hermes was counselled by the god: 'Increase thyself to an immeasurable greatness higher than all height, lower than all depth'; 'Equal thyself to God.' That becomes possible for us because there is in us a centre through which all the threads of the universe are drawn, or a spirit in which the ideations of the divine mind are mirrored; and our imagination in its fiery brooding at last identifies itself with that and in that fusion the mortal reassumes its immortality."

"Yes, but this majestic wisdom was also told by Avatars in the past. Are we not looking for some hitherto unheard-of wisdom?"

Conaire turned to Mark but he was one who spoke little, and he said only:

"I think if Aodh was an Avatar he was an Avatar of freedom. Whether as boy or man he passed by, he seemed to be free like those who have no fears about the morrow, or what he might eat or what he might wear. He had the air of one to whom earth was a gigantic genie who could be trusted to bring what he needed, as that genie did who was slave of the lamp. He looked as if he knew the rocks could put out hands to offer him bread, or the sky would drop down to bring him raiment. He had the air of a king who knows he has many allies and could call them from the silence of the hills. He was like that other Avatar—

When but a child he ran away.

When he passed by me, even as a boy, I felt, that is, my soul within felt, as if it wanted to take off the clothes of the body and become a sky-walker, going where it willed, no longer earth-bound. I think that freedom is what the soul most needs, for here it is slave to such baubles of comfort or praise or profit. It may be Aodh who made me so free that the body seems but a dream wrapt round me, and when I wake in the morning I wonder how I came into so strange a thing. You know I have never had but one idea in what I modelled or carved but the liberation of the spirit. I have an intuition that once the spirit in us was pure and free we would find the universe rushing to us, as a friend might with outstretched hands, ready to pour all its treasures into us. Aodh walked as if he knew the proud earth was bowed before him. But I really cannot tell what I feel." And then, as if abashed at his own unaccustomed talkativeness, the sculptor relapsed awkwardly into silence.

"That is an interpretation that I love," said Conaire. "But the Avatars of old were before Aodh in this. We are finding that the spirit can act through many men and speak with many voices. But there are others who have yet to speak who believe that an immortal walked the same earth as they did, and that they saw him with their own eyes."

He had hardly spoken when Rory, the young musician, began to speak with an eagerness broken at times by the shyness of his youth. They all looked on him with kindness, for a spirit that was ancient with youth seemed to be stammering through the lips of boyhood.

XXIII

"I THINK he came to make life a music; to unseal the music in nature. The universe we see is only a lovely dust raised by the vibration of that music. Aodh we knew as the Fairy Fiddler when he was a boy. He carried that violin with him to the end. Has not every Avatar his symbol, caduceus, lyre or cross! I think Aodh will carry that violin as long as he is in the memory of earth. When he played to us as children he did not only make the feet to dance but the heart. Every bit of us ran to some music. I lay awake at night trying to recapture a music that seemed to lead from that sound to the fountain of all melody. My soul was lifted up and itself became a music, that which lies behind the beating of the heart and the flowing of the blood. We dreamed a great deal, my sister Aileen and I. We sometimes dreamed the same dream and sometimes we went on ways of our own. The dreams I loved most seemed to bring me to some shoreless sea of melody like the voices of unnumbered seas in which stars danced and sang. Once I remembered in dream being laid down eastward, while a voice whispered in my ear, 'Listen to the music, lose yourself in the music,' and under my closed eyelids I looked into my heart, which glowed to a great orb of light, and out of the light came that music, the heart music the Indians call it, and I lost myself in the sound. I could not remember when I woke how far I had climbed up the musical stair of being. But I knew that music, song, was at the root of life. All this dreaming began when the Fairy Fiddler began to pass by us on his wanderings. I tried to make music myself, but there was a magic in Aodh's playing which made it seem a gate in the silence opening to a melody that was innumerable. After I heard him first I began to hear music among the hills, a melody in the aether. I came to think that we were to be changed in our nature; that, along with the infinity of light our eyes can see, there would gradually come the revelation of the universe as sound or music. I think when first we began to see there was only a blindness of light. Then after that we began to distinguish what was near and what was far and the glory of many colours. And so we will first hear that great tone, and after we will know the distant voices of sun, moon and stars, and the carol the flowers make as they grow, and we will not be confused by these innumerable voices of things any more than we are by the innumerable colours and forms which all keep their place in the universe of light. So these voices far and near will keep their places in an infinite harmony, and—and——" The eager boy broke down, confused by the multitude of ideas which thronged for utterance, and for which he had no words. But the voice carried some of the music of which he spoke, and as he drew back, timid after his boldness, Mark, who was his special friend, laid his hand on the hand of the boy in the assurance of another's love for his imagination, and Conaire said:

"In what has just been said there is indeed the sense of something hitherto unheard of. If there ever was on earth before an Avatar revealing the music in the nature of things, the music he awoke has long trembled into silence. Though Apollo is depicted with his lyre, we do not know what songs he may have sung. Though there were those in the past who spoke about the music of the spheres, there was never a world religion with this as its root idea." He would have gone on, but

Olive, who had listened intent on all that had been spoken, stood up and began to speak with an eagerness no less impetuous than that of the young musician.

"You all speak as if there was but one in this wonder of our lives. You forget with Aodh there was Aoife. I listened to everything that was said, and it was beautiful and wonderful those visions of a living nature, or of the imagination climbing into heaven, or the freedom of the soul, or of the music that lies within life. But one Avatar might have revealed such things. Whatever mystery had to be revealed two had to come. In this Aoife was with Aodh. He said to her when they met: 'It is time for the play to begin.' She said: 'I am ready,' speaking of something preconceived and now to be fulfilled. What was the play to reveal? You have given answers according to your nature. You are all beautiful inhuman creatures"—she stamped her foot at them. "You go on some rapt wandering of your own. You have no companions climbing with you into your heavens. There must be an ethic in every revelation of the spirit. What are we to do with each other from day to day? That must be our best wisdom. I am not wise of myself. I never had to fight with dark powers. I have been sheltered by affection. When I was a little girl Paul told me fairy stories, and Felim talked to me about a fairy universe, and I was with Aoife who showed me fairy itself and told me these fairy lands were only pleasure grounds where the soul died in dream. I know but little about Aodh though I think he must be some great one. I was close to Aoife all my life almost, yet she was as much a mystery to me as Aodh to you, and as great a wonder to all who met her. She glowed with an inner light as if her body was but a shade to a golden fire, or as if summer itself had taken form. Through her the ice of many hearts was broken up so that they knew the sweetness of life once more. This is as great a wonder as the opening of visionary eyes. Men are for ever roaming with adventurous minds. We brood with hungry hearts over life. You seek for the new, we try to transmute the old. You exult if you discover a new star, a new starry country. We are happy if a cold heart melts into sympathy. Aoife passed like a gay transfiguring fire through life. She was beset even as a girl by those who desired that beauty to be beside them always. She slipped by them. She could with a word, a laugh, crumble whole lofty Himalayas of pretence, breaking up the moulds of mind in which so many imprison themselves. But she did not drive the soul naked out of the house of its self-imaginings but gave to each a star by which they might be guided. She spoke to others as if they were immortals, as if she saw seraph kings glowing through the dusky rags and tatters of the body. She told me I was to love only the immortal in people, to let none be comrade of my heart but those who had found the immortal in myself. I came to change from my childish delight in the fairy things, who thronged about her when we played long ago in the woods, to a feeling of awe. She grew up within swiftly and beyond me where I could not follow her. She was a being of a different order. Even if my eyes were shut beside her, the light from her made me to glow inwardly. Once I slept in the same room and had a dream which was, I think, more than a dream. There rose out of her sleeping body a glorious creature like the sun for brightness. I did not know where it went or what it did. But I said calmly, as one who knew, to another who was with me in my dream, 'She is one of the Dawn Maidens,' and after that her body to me was only a lovely disguise. I tried to interpret her ways and the swift unreasonable things she did as action by a spirit who saw what I could not see. She was a divine comrade who overlooked none and who heaped precious things on others. I think there must have been this divine companionship between Aodh and Aoife, the companionship of those who know themselves from earth to heaven, and it was such a divine companionship they wished to create. Did they not in the dances they taught, whether by music or motion or by some magic, make men and women so rapt and exalted in their imaginings that they became god and goddess to each other and knew that they must cling to that in each other for evermore? It was so heaven-making a companionship they came to inspire. It is wonderful to think of such a thing, to go on for ever under sun-rich, under star-rich skies, ever falling deeper into the enchantment of the universe, and to know there is no end to it, no end to the lovely things we discover in each other." The girl looked with luminous, questioning eyes at those about her, at Paul her oldest friend, to see if they, if he, understood with what purpose Aodh and Aoife scattered largesse on the soul in their passing. She saw only love-tender eyes, and as if she was satisfied she sank back into her chair.

"Everyone among us has had the gift from heaven that he or she desired," said Conaire; "and you," he turned to Cluborn, "who have come from the New World, who made yourself friend of us all as if you had lived always among us, what meaning has all this to you?"

"The meanings are too great for me. I am like a scribe taking down the words of some infinitely wise person, words which he does not now understand, but on which he may brood hereafter. I was left with wealth, and as I was nothing of myself there seemed to be little I could do but to gather the harvest of past beauty, and I came to the Old World. Someone told me new and lovely things were being fashioned by artists and craftsmen in this region. I began my search. I found myself stirred with the discovery of a new art, a new mood in art. I walked from place to place, and one day I sat down by the roadside. Just before me the road rose to its crest, and then ran downward to a valley I could not see. Beyond the crest of the road there was nothing but a blue sky and far hills misty in light. I heard voices from unseen people coming up from below. I was suddenly quickened by a vibrant music in the voices. Then there rose over the ridge, walking swiftly—the memory will be with me for ever—a woman who moved like the Winged Victory, white garments, sunlit, wind-blown, flowing over shapely limbs, and a man more lordly than I had ever known man to be, with bare head, golden hair rising lion-like over the brows and blown behind him, and eyes fuller of light than the sky. They swept swiftly by me like flames, god and goddess, and the whole universe seemed to my imagination to be with them in their going. I heard a voice as of one who had passed beyond sorrow, who was speaking out of an eternity or fulness of joy: 'Every beating of the wing of time is blessed. For every instant there is a God-born joy.' They went on. I was overpowered by their coming, too blinded by that revelation to rise and go after. I found myself crying out words I had read in some Buddhist tract: 'A fragrance blows from the leaders of the world by which all creatures are intoxicated.' Later I rose to follow a beauty greater than I had sought for or imagined possible. I came after a time to know those I had seen were Aodh and Aoife, and that this truly was the beauty I had come to seek. Yet when I knew this they had passed beyond any knowing of ours. That is why I have gone to every place they have been, and have written down all that was told to me that nothing might be lost. It may be some other brooding on all may come to a more profound wisdom than any of us and give the true story of Aodh and Aoife to the world."

XXIV

"I WONDER," said Felim, "what was implied in those shining sentences: 'Every beating of the wing of time is blessed. For every instant there is a God-born joy'? Is it that for every one of us there is a God-imagined path from which we have erred and strayed, and if we follow that path we are happy always and are beautiful to others? I have watched people for enchanted moments when every movement was rhythmical and they were in a more lovely harmony with nature and each other than the riders on the Parthenon. Only yesterday I saw a girl racing over the sands, and girl, sands, tumbling waters, light, cloud and shadow seemed not separate but one thing, as if some purity of the girl's being made it possible for the master of every art to draw her into a harmony with his other imaginations. I tried to put into words that God-guided enchantment:

"Thou slender of limb; thou lightness;
Wild grace that flies
Over the shining sands
Under cloud-brilliant skies,

What beauty flies within thee,
Sped from what skies?

"Thee for an instant
The God possesses,
Is joy in thy fleet limbs,
Gay feet and flying tresses.
His lovely thought of thee, the Artist
Delights in and caresses.

"Thou shalt remember hereafter
Through sorrowful years,
That wonder of all thy moments
And pine for through tears,
This moment that shall be for thee
A fountain of tears.

"I might have been happier in my prophecy," he said. "I only thought then of her falling out of the divine procession and the sorrow of it."

"Here is one," said Conaire of Cluborn, "who came last into our company, and from far away, and yet his fleeting vision of Aodh and Aoife in their secret joy may have in it as great a revelation as long brooding has brought to any of us. What was it you felt? That their being seemed to rise out of a shoreless sea of joy. I do not know whether there are such beings in the universe, but we are for ever brooding on such an eternal joy, we are for ever seeking a way to it in our hearts. To feel this was true about any is a great magic."

"There are many who felt this enchantment," said Cluborn. "I found a house Aodh and Aoife had entered for an hour. The man who told me the tale said they filled the room with such a magic of light and loveliness that he had made a shrine of the room. He would let none enter it. He himself meditates long before he opens the door of the room, and he stands there silently trying to re-create in his heart the magic of the beauty he had known."

"That is coming nigh idolatry," said Felim. "We shall next hear of prayers to the two, or of girls supplicating Aoife for happiness in love."

"The story has gone into the world," Conaire said. "It cannot be recalled. It will take a thousand forms in the soul, and it will be well if there is nothing more sinister than a girl praying for herself and her lover."

The old man had become thoughtful.

"The story of Aodh and Aoife has started some who were naturally spiritual upon more heavenly travelling. But what will it bring to others? There never yet was a fire which did not cast dark shadows of itself. I wonder what dark counterpart of itself the story will create in some obscene souls."

They then began to speak of other things.

Mark brought out the plans of the temple he had made for the American. They were unrolled on the table and praised for their beauty. Here Cluborn desired to bring together everything born out of the quickening of the spirit in that region. Here were to be placed the art of Paul, Mark and many others, the works of poets, dramatists and imaginative craftsmen. They were talking about the divine innocence of some paintings done in a little colony of mystics, when Paul, near to the open door, heard footsteps. He moved to the doorway and saw there a man he knew a little and liked not at all. He was one of the famous story-tellers of his time. When he saw the artist, he spoke to him in the soft caressing voice of those who are accustomed to speak to women more than to men.

"No. I will not come in. I was passing and heard you lived here. This is but to call and say farewell. We have seen you but little for some years. You are a hater of cities, I hear. Your paintings I have seen, of course. Very distinguished. But rather remote, that stellar illumination in all of them. You know I am a creature of this world. I only came to this country looking for local colour, a romantic background for a tale which I think will be my masterpiece. You living here must, of course, be familiar with the story of the two who disappeared. A beautiful woman who might, I believe, have been a queen, met a peasant poet or musician. You understand the attraction opposite grades of society have for each other. The romance of it! They went rambling together in a country of lakes and hills. Of course she became his mistress. But none here believe it. They get angry at the thought. They will have it the companionship was platonic. But you and I understand life. We know that platonic affection is the most enchanting approach to bodily love. People imagine wonderful things about each other. They seem to be groping for the heavens and suddenly find themselves in each other's arms. Religion, philosophy, poetry, music, all the arts indeed, beget lovely phantoms who lead us delicately to a simple act. We feel while possessing the beloved that fairy or goddess has come to us from their skies. Life has given me a tale better than any I ever imagined. Oh, I will make it beautiful, the tale of these two, Aodh and Aoife. What names for romance! What a setting for love, these mountains! these woods! How much more poetical than the hotel! I will send you this greatest of my love stories when it is printed. I know you will like it better than anything I have yet written. Well, after hail, it is now farewell."

He made a gesture of departure. The subtly insinuating, self-caressing voice ceased. The pale face turned away. Paul had listened without a word while his visitor was speaking. Then he turned within. The young musician's face was white, his eyes dark with anger. The girl was shuddering as if at some apparition of incredible and uncomprehended evil. Felim was exhausting all the demoniac resources of speech.

"That thing has worms slinking through its veins, not blood. It would pollute earth to bury him in it. He ought to be dropped off the planet with demons clawing him all the way to the bottomless pit. May nightmares squat on his chest, nightmares with sticky tongues passing him down their throats to blazing furnaces. How could you be still while he oozed out that leprosy of imagination? A word and we would have been at him like hounds."

"Do not speak of him. Do not think of him!" the girl cried passionately. "We grow like what we hate."

"Oh, but—" the poet protested, and then:

"Yes, you are right. In my rage at him I became a devil, and I had been climbing into heaven a moment before. How can I grow wings again!"

"No, do not let us forget him," said Conaire. "His interpretation of the story of Aodh and Aoife has a wisdom for us. Has any beauty been in the world which was not pursued by beasts? How rarely does any beauty enter the soul where there are not red goblins snatching at it, to make out of it more beautiful shapes for their own evil, turning the divine to infernal uses, sweetening some dark delight."

"I remember," said Felim, "Gregor telling us he dared not because of his past allow himself the luxury of dream, lest when he came back from his heaven he might find devils waiting for him in the pit. He had to cling to the austere opposite of all he had been."

"But on that night of his death he told me," said Paul, "that he found he could permit himself to dream. The old devils in him were too feeble and famished to stir. Dear Michael, I wonder if he could share in our symposium how he would interpret the tale."

"What we might now speculate about is, in what way the story will be refashioned by the imagination of the world. Not only the lecherous but many of finer nature will weave about it their own fantasy. Let us remember the austere profundities uttered by great Avatars and what was built on them. How the story of Jesus was smothered with monstrous growths. Some with a sadistic emotion brooded upon the torture of the God until the pain itself became a thing to be adored. There grew up a luxury of anguished emotion. Pain, if it comes naturally to us here, if it is endured with resignation, brings its own nobility. But to seek it for its own sake, that is devilish. The brooding on agonies, martyrdoms and crucifixions leads the soul into sinister by-ways. Out of that brooding upon the tortured God was born the mentality which made the dark ages hideous with religious persecutions, with the rack, the stake and the martyr's fire. The way out of that had to be by the drawn sword. The fantasies of great poets, too, like Dante and Milton, deflect us in another way from the true, for they send the imagination outward, whereas the aim of all high religion is to throw the imagination inward to being. Once the tale of Aodh and Aoife has entered the imagination of the world, the myth may grow prodigiously. The least incident recorded may excite artist or poet or story-teller; and, finally, what is born out of the tale may have as little relation to the original as Dante's *Inferno* has to the Sermon on the Mount. We cannot stay this growth, though we can foresee it. The Chinese sage Lâo-tze said, 'To see things in germ, this I call intelligence.' It was to divine the outcome of all this we began our symposium. You cannot be confident that what glows with so pure a light in your minds will not multiply images and shadows of itself in others until it has lost all spiritual significance. We can understand why ancient Greek and Egyptian made mysteries of their most spiritual truths. These were communicated only after there had been purifications and vows that they would never be revealed. They knew that to spread wide the noblest ideas would be to degrade them, as Homer, a great secular genius, degraded the gods. Plato, who had the reverence of an initiate for the truth, would have exiled him from his ideal republic. To give sacred mysteries to the mob is like a man casting the most beautiful of his children into the streets to be degraded by prostitution."

XXV

"If the light casts so dark a shadow," asked Paul, "what does a descent from Heaven give to us?"

"When the soul enters a higher heaven in its own nature it must have insight into lower deeps. We descend into these, not to surrender to them, not to be overcome, but to bring about a harmony or fusion of opposites. I think only by this fusion of opposites does the soul itself become strong. We cannot go from earth leaving behind us untransmuted the elements and forces the soul had gathered about itself, the dross and slime of its life."

"I sigh at the long, long labour," said Felim. "But I will try to think of that transmutation as making a heart friend out of an enemy."

"Let us return," said Conaire, "to the interpretations of Aodh and Aoife which have been made. If they were Avatars—they certainly moved among us with mysterious power—they differ from all Avatars of whom we have knowledge in this, that they left behind them no body of doctrine. No one has discovered sayings of Aodh or Aoife which, put together, might form a scripture. Whatever has been told about them, all that is wonderful, has come from vision or intuition of the onlooker. To interpret we have to go inward, to see things unseen by the bodily eyes, to hear things unheard by the sensual ear. The Avatars who went before had disciples to whom they spoke about creation, the architecture of the heavens. They left a wisdom about life and death, what to do and what not to do. Multitudes pondered over it all, and out of that pondering came theologies, philosophies, ethic, psychology, literature, arts, and last a civilisation. The immaterial soul finally cast substantial shadows of itself in brick and mortar. Men were thus impelled to continue their labours in the world. But what are we to think of Avatars who come to us and do nothing in the manner of their forerunners? We surmise a divinity within them. Whoever came nigh them had a quickening of soul. It became incandescent as torches set ablaze by the touch of fire. Why were these two so great, and yet so secret and silent? This secrecy and silence must have profound meanings. It was said of the Popol Vuh that its wisdom was hidden from him who sees with his eyes, who hears with his ears. They were like·that. Because of this I ask myself was it in their plan to create a civilisation at all? They guarded their mystery. They played like two divine children, careless of our questioning, and only intuition can discover the meaning of that play which enchanted us. Was it in the plan we should be allured to build a new civilisation out of a new culture. I think not. Why? Because I believe we are past the high noon of time and are drawing to its twilight. It is time for men to leave their labours here. Earth is crowded with the ruins of the cities they have built. They have come to age in soul. Even when the body is young and desirous, if we meditate on what we do we grow listless. We have lived through too many empires. Is there any mood of the heart told even by the great masters in literature which is not stale to us? Even from human love the enchantment has gone. If we are not pursuing the chase, if in stillness we turn inward, we find only a grey Eros without desire dwelling in the heart. Has there not been this earth-weariness among us all? Have we not come out of the world and found our happiness only pondering by the margin of the Great Deep?

It was to people with this age of the soul that the avatars came, but as they passed by us, they made us feel we yet might bathe in some fountain and come to an immortality of youth? They left no wisdom for moralist or philosopher to dilate into systems which as they grew could only enslave us. They gave us no ethic, no commandment to do or forbear. Such things are not natural. They do violence to the soul, begetting exaltations followed by despairs. No one can state a moral law which is sufficient for the infinite complexities of life. But as we grow nigher to deep own-being, our passions drop away from us. We act with tenderness to all for we enter the great unity of all-life. What we do is in natural accord with that divine nature which takes possession of us. The consequences of our acts, then, are like a fragrance blown over the world. It is time for us to go homeward, to climb the terraces of being by which we descended to this world. Do any of us feel inspired to labour at another civilisation. Those who came to us gave us nothing but the certainty that they were divinities and a longing to be like them, to be with them whither they are gone. Nothing about them can be proven outwardly. It was only the visionaries who knew them, who were dazzled, seeing through the mask of the body some flashing of the plumes of the bird of paradise. I doubt if they were killed. I think they went inward and homeward. Gregor was the only martyr. Whatever they were, their secret remains inviolate from those who see with their eyes and hear only with their ears. Maybe to those who open those secret radiant gateways to light of which Aoife spoke, the mystery will be revealed. But it will be found there, not here."

"Was I wrong in my thought to build a temple of the arts inspired by them?" the American asked.

"I do not think so. All that will be gathered there, the painting, the sculpture and whatever else, will not draw men out of themselves, but will light the candle of vision within the psyche."

"What are we to do, then? How are we to climb those terraces of being you speak of when the avatars have told us nothing?"

"Are you certain about this? They did not speak in words, but did they not speak in other ways? Did they not create light within us? Did we not feel them in our very spirits? Can we say that they have departed and left not a gift behind until we use the candle of vision and explore the upper chambers of the soul? We might discover all the ways to these were lit. The links binding us to earth have been loosened, while the links binding us to each other have been made stronger. We tend to overflow into each other. What one knows all of us soon know. To one there came the vision of nature as a vast ocean of being bathing heart and mind. With another the universe is revealed as a music. A third feels the free gay movement of the upper airs, and the girders of the soul which bind it to earth are slackened. Another is moved to be co-worker with that imagination which everywhere is making, sustaining and re-creating the world. Another feels that being as a profound tenderness enveloping all that lives. All have been raised above themselves and all have in some way imparted their vision to the rest. Is not this true? Do we not surmise swiftly the desire or thought in the heart of another even when the friend is distant? Do we not come to each other without outer asking? Did any send messages to bring us here? Did not our friend think of us and we came? To climb into heaven might be difficult for one alone. But when there are seven or eight we will and aspire with the strength of all. At last, like adventurers who have found a marvellous country beyond the seas and who settle there, we may make firm our place in that other world and be able to know each other there in whatever way the psyche appears to the psyche. I think, too, we will find others there inspired like us to such heavenly climbing. At last the bonds of matter will, I think, wear thin so that our life shall be more there than here. We may be able at last to live there completely, finding in it an ark of refuge from this world which our men of science tell us is growing old like the moon. Do you not like the idea of leaving the world by our own strength? I have always thought it an indignity that we should be thrust out of the body by the falling in of its rafters, or the crumbling of its walls of clay, being outcast against our will. There must be a lordly way out of the body by one of those secret radiant gateways into light. If we do not find this way, I think we must return again and again to the body until we have mastered the secret of death and can take that lordly way out by our own will."

While the elder had been speaking, Paul had sunken into one of those visionary moods which had become habitual with him. In that visionary mood he saw in the centre of the circle in which they sat a light flashing like a diamond. From that light, as waves might ripple from a flung stone, its glow dilated until it enveloped them all. For an instant there was that light only, and then in another instant a Titan figure was there glowing as if it had been a shape cast in fire. He knew that figure, though transfigured, the lion-like mane of golden hair, or was it flame, which rose above the brows, and the eyes that looked out of eternity. Swiftly it swept a hand round the circle, and Paul saw where the hand moved a light ran from heart to heart linking them as by a chain of fire. In another instant the royal phantom had vanished and the glow had gone inward. There was a silence in the room, a silence which was not physical, a silence of intent and listening souls. No one asked of another whether they had seen anything or of what they had been aware. They were raised above themselves, needing that silence for understanding. A voice would have drawn them outward. There were no voices. Each needed that quiet for himself, or the chain of fire that linked heart to heart had made them all for the moment one mood, one being.

XXVI

After a time the old man began again. His voice seemed to come from far away.

"It is strange that I who am old should yet feel in myself strength and understanding for so great an adventure. The world has become changed for me, as if I had raced back from age to childhood and its heart-charmed country. When I was a boy earth, all nature indeed, seemed tender to me, a presence which melted about me as a nurse who loves her children, plays with them, answering all their demands. To my fantasy the streams then babbled with laughter fed from lovely and hidden springs. Even the gay stars from their towers nodded at me, clapping their elfin hands above my play. When I grew up and became a man, the earth had become solid and nature opaque. Now in my age nature has become transparent once more—melted toward me in some more infinitely majestic way. I feel made young again so that I can undertake that great journey. We have all moved in soul into some new region where we will find each other in some new guise and we will not need to speak each other's names as we do here, but come to profounder intimacies. Perhaps spirit may flow into spirit, and this not with ourselves alone but with many others, so we shall grow into a myriad wisdom."

"If we are going inward," cried Felim, "how shall we know each other there? I do not know myself when I dream. How shall I know you? Rory I might know if I heard a music, and Paul I shall know for he has long been able to make me see his imaginations. How could I know Olive unless she came to me as a silver glow with innumerable stars in it? Or Cluborn unless by a friendliness to all creatures? Maybe we shall be raised above ourselves, transfigured into some divine counterpart of ourselves! And what does going inward mean? I have had my glimpses of a world of light. But is that going inward? Is it not rather going outward to another more lovely Maya? Going inward must mean a miraculous change if not vision but being is dilated. We must feel stirring within life some motions of the great deep."

"Is there not some place in that sphere next to us where we could keep tryst?" Olive spoke impetuously. "Where do you go, Paul, when you shut your eyes and run away from us? You can make Felim see what you see. And I have seen what you imagine often without your telling. You could give to us a place not here but there where we might meet. What does it matter if it be but an imagination if we can find our way there in soul!"

"I will try," said Paul. He sat with shut eyes. His face was set with intensity of will. He was evoking in himself memory of a vision. His head turned slightly to one after another, as one who makes a lit candle to touch with its flame a circle of unlit candles. There began to glow in each the vision of a vast hall with high marvellous pillars, a hall lit with a delicate golden air.

"Oh, I know that place!" cried the girl.

"I know it," said Felim.

"And I, and I," came from one after another.

"I was outcast once from its light when I woke," said the poet. "I had seen wonderful things there I knew, but I could not bring them back. What a place to keep tryst in! Is it one of those temples Socrates spoke of in that divine world which is all around us, temples wherein the gods do truly dwell?

What are we to do? When do we keep tryst there? If I cannot go with my waking consciousness, I will be there surely in soul while I sleep.

"The night after to-morrow is Midsummer Eve. The barriers between earth and heaven are fragile. Let us try to be with each other there. We can meet after and tell what we remember. Once we have surety that we can meet in soul we shall have taken the first step in the great journey."

They were all gay at the thought of so great adventure. They felt a fresh spiritual intimacy. They were conscious that they were knit to each other as the climbers of high mountains are. If one slipped, the others would hold him fast.

"We must go now. We have many miles to walk," said Mark.

Felim and the young musician went with him. They made gestures of farewell silently, as those do who know that departure is not farewell and that space is but a myth to soul.

Paul, Olive, Conaire and Cluborn watched for a while the figures fading in the summer night. Conaire and his New World visitor turned to Conaire's home. Paul and the girl walked slowly after them. The night was luminous. They could see from the hill road the earth, wrinkled with hill and hollow, lying like a vast sleeping creature. The lakes in the hollows glowed like dim moonstones. Paul and his companion did not speak. They who were closer to each other than any in the world beside were yet free, and could take lonely journeys in soul sure that they would not lose the way back to each other. They stood for a while at the crest of the hill road. It was there the Avatars had met and gone on their radiant journey together. In that pause of quietness Paul became aware that the years had changed him, that he had come to be within that life which as a boy he had seen nodding at him through the transparency of air or earth. For many years he had peered through that veil, but he himself, except for moments which were so transient that he was hardly aware of them until they were gone, had been outside the heavenly circle. Now something was living and breathing in him, interpenetrating consciousness, a life which was an extension of the life that breathed through those dense infinitudes. He could not now conceive of himself apart from that great unity. He knew he was, however humbly, one of the heavenly household. In that new exaltation the lights above, the earth below, were but motions of a life that was endless. He almost felt the will that impelled the earth on which he stood on its eternal round. Through earth itself as through a dusky veil the lustre of its vitality glowed. It shimmered with ethereal colour. Space about him was dense with innumerable life. He felt an inexpressible yearning to be molten into that, into all life. He thought of that great adventure he and his friends were beginning, and what transfigurations in life and nature it would mean. What climbing of endless terraces of being! He knew out of what anguish of body and soul, through what dark martyrdoms, come the resurrection and the life, but he thought of these in peace. At last he came back to earth and to his companion. She was still brooding as he had been, her face lifted up to the skies, intent on the same depths. She was unconscious of the one by her side, and at that moment he loved her more in forgetting than in remembering him.

THE END

www.ingramcontent.com/pod-product-compliance
Lightning Source LLC
LaVergne TN
LVHW090941080826
845145LV00003B/848
* 9 7 8 1 5 9 7 3 1 3 0 2 5 *